"COLLINWOOD CAN BE A PLACE OF GREAT OPPORTUNITY FOR YOU. IT CAN ALSO OFFER YOU GREAT DANGER."

Despite the warning, ballerina Diana Samson is looking forward to her stay at Collinwood, where her dance company is to develop and present a new ballet. When she meets Barnabas Collins, she is even more pleased with the situation, for she soon falls in love with him.

Yet the warning comes true all too soon. Diana is in terrible danger—but from whom? Is her attacker a human being, or the legendary Collinwood ghost?

If Barnabas is to save her life, he must find the answer to these questions. But the police suspect Barnabas himself . . . and if the killer is a ghost, who knows whether it possesses greater powers than Barnabas?

If you are unable to obtain these books from your local dealer, they may be ordered directly from the publisher, for 50¢ per book plus 10¢ per copy to cover postage and handling.

Paperback Library
Department B
315 Park Avenue South
New York, New York 10010

Barnabas Collins and the Mysterious Ghost

By Marilyn Ross

PAPERBACK LIBRARY
New York

PAPERBACK LIBRARY EDITION

First Printing: January, 1970

Paperback Library is a division of Coronet Communications, Inc.
Its trademark, consisting of the words "Paperback Library" accompanied by an open book, is registered in the United States Patent Office. *Coronet Communications, Inc., 315 Park Avenue South, New York, N.Y. 10010.*

CHAPTER ONE

Whenever ballet star Diana Samson heard the strains of that lovely yet haunting waltz, she was reminded of Collinwood and the eerie happenings of that summer. Waiting in the wings of the New York State Theater for her entrance cue in Stefan Emmon's ballet success, *Roxanna,* she found herself caught up in the ghostly memories brought back so vividly by the lilting waltz theme.

It had been on the Collinwood estate in a village on the Maine seacoast that Stefan Emmon's original ballet had first been produced. And there as a member of the Mary Wentworth Ballet Company Diana had spent a summer season filled with romance and sheer terror that she would probably remember for all her days!

The ancient stone chapel about a half-mile from the brooding dark mansion known as Collinwood had been taken over by the elderly ballet star, Mary Wentworth, and her troupe for a summer season of ballet. Elizabeth Stoddard, who presided over Collinwood, had given the use of the chapel, a nearby farmhouse and its barns to the gallant little dance group that had temporarily been beset by financial problems.

Elizabeth had also offered the principals of the company, including Diana, free room and board at Collinwood. It was a generous gesture on the part of this daughter of the Collins clan and promised to offer the visitors during the tourist season in Collinsport an unusual attraction. Admission to the ballet performances in the old chapel was to be kept at the lowest possible prices.

In the space of little more than a year following the summer season in Maine, Diana had found stardom in the title role of *Roxanna.* But the girl who had first appeared in the ballet and whirled gracefully about the stage of the murky old chapel theater had been murdered. Murdered by a mysterious ghost that had haunted the vine and moss-covered chapel and brought all of them face to face with a horrifying phantom from the past!

Diana herself had been touched by the invisible

skeleton hands and had more than one close call with death. Yet those warm summer days of relentless rehearsal under the keen and merciless eye of eighty-year-old Mary Wentworth had gradually molded her into a ballet dancer of outstanding grace and style. The elderly head of the troupe seemed determined to find a talent among them on whom to graft her own talents—someone who could carry on the Mary Wentworth legend. Though Diana hadn't guessed it at the time, she had been the one the old lady had selected.

But something else had helped forge Diana's talents to perfection, she knew this better than anyone. In addition to the grueling work of the hot, sunny days, there had been the nightmarish encounters of the cool, dark nights. And there had been the experience of love and heartbreak. For all her memories of those days and nights of challenge, adventure and terror had been dominated by the handsome, caped figure of one man, Barnabas Collins!

It had began when she took the taxi from the bus depot in Ellsworth to Collinsport and the Collinwood estate on the cliffs. The driver, a middle-aged garrulous type with a stubble of gray beard on his tanned face, and a battered driver's cap surmounting a thatch of silver gray hair, was familiar with everything and everyone in the area.

As the taxi moved swiftly along the two-lane highway, skirting the ocean, past weathered frame houses and the occasional gas station and restaurant catering to the summer tourist, he talked freely about Collinwood and its owners.

"Collins family have had that land since the port was established. A mighty old family," he said. "Elizabeth and her brother, Roger, are the two living there and running the fishing business now. Of course they've both got children. Elizabeth has a daughter, Carolyn, pretty little thing works in the village in one of the gift shops in summer. And Roger has a boy, David, about twelve years old."

From the back seat of the taxi Diana said, "So there are some young people in the house."

The driver nodded, keeping his eyes on the winding road. "Yep. But you don't think of Collinwood as a place for youngsters. It's a brooding old house. Folk tell a lot of strange stories about it. Roger has a governess taking charge of the boy and also a little girl named Amy Jennings, who is staying there. Governess is a nice girl by name of Maggie Evans."

Diana smiled to herself. She was a diminutive, pretty girl with golden hair and lovely blue eyes, the focus of interest in a small-featured intelligent face. The way the driver was rattling off names made it hard for her to keep track of his account of the Collins family.

"I understand it's a forty-room house," she said. "I and some of the others in the ballet company are going to be living there with the family."

The man at the wheel chuckled. "You won't be crowded none, and that's for sure. Some of the wings at Collinwood are shut off and never used. That is, unless you count the ghosts who are supposed to roam around in them."

It was the first hint she'd had that Collinwood was haunted. Sitting in the back seat of the car on this warm, summer afternoon with the sun flooding in through the car windows, it was odd that she should immediately have a reaction to the driver's words. But she did. It was as if icy fingers had slithered down her spine.

A tiny frown came to her face. "What about ghosts at Collinwood?"

The gray-haired driver gave her a quick grin over his shoulder. "You'll hear plenty about them if you live in that old house. You can take your pick. Local folk won't venture near there after dark if they can help it. There's the Phantom Mariner said to walk Widows' Hill, not to mention the ghost of Anya Collins or the vampires and werewolves more than one has claimed to see."

Diana was startled. "You make it sound as if the estate is a rendezvous for dark spirits?"

The driver made an expert turn on a sharp curve of the narrow asphalt road that seemed to run along the shore. They had skirted the village of Collinsport and were now on the more sparsely settled coastal route leading to the estate of Collinwood. At this point the road ran close to the high cliffs that came to a crest near the mansion of dark shadows.

"More than one queer tale has been told about Collinwood," the driver assured her. "And a lot of the Collins

7

family are strange ones. Right now there is a cousin, name of Barnabas, visiting from England. He's a pleasant enough sort, but wears clothes you'd never see around here. Always in a kind of caped coat and carries a fancy cane with a silver head shaped like a wolf's head."

Her eyebrows raised. "Sounds like a very distinguished type."

"You could call him that, Miss," the man at the wheel agreed. "He lives in what is called the old house. It was the first Collinwood and is located part way between the main house and the family cemetery. Has a servant with him, rough sort by the name of Hare. You see him around days with a surly look on his face. But you never see the main gent, Barnabas Collins, except after dusk. Gossip is he roams around the graveyard by himself at night."

Again a chill went through her. "What would make him do that?"

"Who knows?" the driver said. "I told you the Collins family are a strange lot. Some people say he's one of those fellas who dabble in black magic. Me, I say, he's just an odd ball. We got plenty of them in this part of Maine." He chuckled.

"But you say this Barnabas is a visitor?"

"Yep. Comes here every so often. Women all think he's handsome. Some nights he visits the Blue Whale Tavern, and all the local girls try to get his eye."

"He sounds extremely interesting," Diana said. "Our ballet company is going to give performances in the chapel on the estate. And Mrs. Stoddard is giving us the farmhouse and barns for living and rehearsal quarters."

The gray-haired driver nodded. "So I've heard! Just what kind of a shindig is this here ballet business? We never had anything like it here before."

"Ballet is telling a story through dance. Instead of saying the words as in a play, we use pantomime and dance to tell our story to a proper musical accompaniment."

"Then it's like a kind of show with a story?"

"Yes," she agreed. "I guess most of our people are here by now. I had a television engagement in New York and it kept me late getting here."

"Yep. I been driving quite a few of them from Ellsworth," the driver agreed. "Seem to be a weird lot, if

8

you'll excuse me sayin' so. Not that you're like them. But the men have long hair and the women all have their hair pulled back in ponytails and dress like gypsies. A lot of hippies, I'd call them. And they're not big, either men or women."

Diana laughed. "It's true that ballet people tend to be small in size. But don't put us down as mere hippies. Most of us have studied long and hard to be dancers. And don't think we're awkward on the stage if we seem to slouch around. It's strange, but most female ballet dancers have a flat-footed walk."

"That sure enough describes the ones I've seen," the gray-haired man at the wheel agreed. "I guess I'll have to come and take a look at your show after you open."

"We're doing a new ballet written by the musical director of the company, a young man named Stefan Emmon, who, I believe, has true genius even if he's a little morose and strange. It's called *Roxanna*."

"Sounds like a girl's name," the driver ventured, slowing down as they turned from the main highway into a tree-shaded side road that was even more narrow. "This road is part of the Collinwood estate," he informed her.

"Then we should be there soon?"

"You'll see the house in a couple of minutes."

"Where is the chapel?"

"On this side of the main house," the driver said, jerking his head to the right. "The chapel, the farmhouse and the old cemetery are all close together beyond the field on the right."

Diana stared thoughtfully out the side window. "But you mentioned an old house and a cemetery beyond it where this Barnabas Collins is supposed to walk after dark?"

"Not the same cemetery," the man at the wheel said at once. "The one by the chapel is the old cemetery and the one by the first Collinwood is what we call the new one though it dates back more than a century. The estate has been here a long while."

"That is apparent," she agreed.

"Ahead is Collinwood," he announced.

Then she saw the great sprawling house with imposing gardens and shrubbery. It seemed the most august and imposing structure she'd seen in the area. It had a number of tall, dark chimneys streaking up to the sky. And she was ready to admit that there was something ominous about it.

"People comin' to your show can use the back road," the driver said. "That way they can keep away from the main house, Widows' Hill, and all the rest. Lucky, too, since a lot of folk won't venture near the main house after dark."

"It surely is," she agreed, puzzled by his words and putting them down to local superstition.

"You'll be getting off at the main house?" he asked.

"Please," she said as the taxi came to a halt by the entrance door.

The driver opened the car door for her and then busied himself with getting her luggage from the trunk. Diana moved towards the entrance of Collinwood, where a slim, gracious-looking, dark-haired woman stood in the doorway to greet her.

"I'm Elizabeth Stoddard," the older woman said with a smile. "Welcome to Collinwood, Miss Samson."

They shook hands as the taxi driver brought her bags to the steps. Diana paid him and he thanked her with a knowing look on his weathered face. As he returned to his car, Elizabeth Stoddard ushered Diana into the house.

Diana was much impressed by the big mansion. The hall was high-ceilinged and cool. On one of the walls was a huge oil painting of a dark man with handsome, melancholy features, and whose eyes seemed to follow her from the canvas as she moved about.

"What a striking portrait!" she exclaimed.

Elizabeth nodded. "Most people think so," she said. "It was painted more than a century ago by an artist whose name we do not know. The subject was an ancestor of ours, who lived in the old house and later went to England. As a matter of fact a descendant of his who much resembles him is visiting us now."

Diana smiled at her. "You must mean Barnabas Collins."

Elizabeth showed surprise. "I do. But how would you know?"

"Very easily. The taxi driver mentioned you had a cousin from London staying here."

10

The older woman looked thoughtful. "Barnabas has a striking personality. He has caught the attention of the locals."

"I gathered that," she said, thinking it discreet to say none of the rather uncomplimentary things the driver had mentioned about Barnabas and the family in general. She could understand that the villagers would be awed by the people in this mansion and their way of life. It was bound to be different from what they knew.

"Miss Wentworth is in her room upstairs," Elizabeth said. "I have just taken her up some tea. After I've shown you to your room I'll take you to her."

Diana followed the woman up the stairs and then down a shadowed corridor to a comfortable bedroom overlooking the ocean. It was furnished in a turn-of-the-century fashion with a canopied bed which gave it added charm. The carpet was oriental and thick to the step.

Elizabeth smiled at her. "The bathroom is just a few doors down. I hope you'll be comfortable here."

"I'm sure I shall," Diana assured her. "I think it's wonderful of you to take our company in as you have. Otherwise, I'm sure, we might have had to disband."

"I was glad to do it," the older woman said. "I have always been a great admirer of Mary Wentworth since the days when as a young girl I first saw her. She was one of the great talents in ballet and must be an inspiring director."

"She is," Diana said.

"She tells me she has bookings to keep the company occupied beginning in the fall, and that the summer season you will be offering here will serve to carry you over. The village will benefit culturally by having the company perform and it should draw a good many extra tourists."

"I sincerely hope so," Diana said. "The new ballet we'll be presenting is simple in theme and style. It should be popular. I'm looking forward to seeing the chapel."

"It's only a short walk from here along a lane that begins by the barns," Elizabeth said. "Most of your people are staying at the farmhouse. But I'm delighted to have Miss Wentworth and some of you here."

"I've looked forward to the cool Maine weather after New York," Diana said.

Elizabeth smiled. "It can get hot here, but it always cools off at night." She went over and pulled the drapes open a little more so that the room had better light from its two windows. Turning to Diana again, she said, "Our handy man, Matt Morgan, will bring up your luggage in a few minutes. Meanwhile, perhaps you'd like to see Miss Wentworth?"

Diana smiled. "Yes. I'd like that."

Elizabeth led her out into the corridor again and down a few doors to another room overlooking the ocean. The door was partly ajar and Diana saw the famous Mary Wentworth seated in an armchair before a portable tea table. As the owner of the house took her in, the old ballet star glanced up with an expression of mild surprise which at once became a smile.

"Ah, Diana," she said in her thin voice, "so you have arrived at last." Mary Wentworth was ramrod straight for eighty, extremely thin with blue-veined hands, and had a round, wrinkled, very-white face. Her hair was pure white and coiled in a skimpy bun at the nape of her neck. Only her small, deep-set eyes remained a snapping, youthful black.

"I couldn't get away from New York until last night," she explained.

"Well, you are here now and that is what matters," the old woman said. She indicated a chair. "Sit down and join me in having tea, girl." And including Elizabeth in her glance, she added, "Perhaps you will also join us, Mrs. Stoddard?"

Elizabeth smiled her refusal. "Thank you, not now. I'm expecting the children and their governess back from the beach soon. I want to be downstairs when they arrive." And with a pleasant nod, she went out and left the two of them alone in the big room.

Mary Wentworth waved Diana to sit down. "Mrs. Stoddard is a fine woman. Thanks to her generosity, we shall be able to properly rehearse and stage *Roxanna*."

From the chair opposite the aged woman Diana said, "I'm terribly excited about it. I think it is a fine piece of work."

Mary poured her a cup of tea and passed it to her. "Stefan has a remarkable talent," she agreed. "But the

12

ballet does need certain changes and work. He is such a moody young man I find him difficult to manage. If he were not our musical director and half-brother to our star, Mavis Norrad, I'd be inclined to give up the project."

"That would be a pity."

"I know," Mary said. "So I will attempt to reason with him. We have already begun some of the ensemble rehearsals. Now that you are here, we shall begin rehearsing the principal roles. You will have the second female lead."

Diana nodded. She had wondered what part she'd have in this new ballet. Since the lead called for a young girl, she'd hoped she might be chosen. But auburn-haired Mavis Norrad was only in her early thirties and could play the part easily. It was strange that she always thought of Mavis as older. Perhaps because her husband, the male star of the ballet, Peter Norrad, was in his late forties.

"What part will Alex Carter do?" Diana asked. Alex was about her own age and another prominent talent in the group.

The old woman across from her gave her a shrewd glance. "Alex will play the young lover. And Peter Norrad will do the role of the Satanic stranger. It should make a well-balanced cast. You will also understudy the female lead."

"Thank you," she said. This was an excellent opportunity for her. She had wondered whether she'd be allowed to do this as well as play a large part.

Mary's face creased in a smile. "I am not overlooking your talents, girl. Never fear. I want *Roxanna* to be the crowning point of my career and make our small company famous."

"Are all the other principals here in the main house?"

"Yes," the old woman said, sipping her tea. "And what an interesting house Collinwood is. So suitable that we should mount our production of the ballet here in this phantom-ridden place."

Diana stared at her. She was startled to hear her so plainly describe the mansion as haunted. She said, "Do you really feel there are spirits here?"

The lively black eyes gleamed with secret knowledge. "I have always been sensitive to the presence of voices and bodies from the other world. And I can hear the soft

13

whispers and the furtive footsteps in every dark corner of this old house."

Diana put down her cup. "I find that amazing. On the way here the taxi driver hinted that the local people feel Collinwood is a haunted place."

"And they are right," Mary said with satisfaction. "So, it is an ideal atmosphere for us to bring our new ballet to life."

"When will we have our first rehearsal? I'd like to see the chapel where the performances will be given."

The old woman smiled. "I like your enthusiasm. We'll begin rehearsals in the morning, but the chapel is always open. You can go over there after dinner and look at it."

"I must."

"The farmhouse is within sight of it and you will find the rest of the company there," she said.

Diana got up. "I must go back to my room and unpack."

The old woman nodded. "Keep your eyes open, girl," she advised. "This can be a place of great opportunity for you. It can also offer you great danger. Keep that in mind."

She frowned. "Danger?"

"Ghosts can be jealous," was the eighty-year-old woman's enigmatic comment.

Diana left the star feeling puzzled. Mary Wentworth seemed to possess some strange knowledge concerning the weird old mansion. Knowledge she was not ready to impart at the moment. The talk of the cab driver and the comments of the veteran ballet star seemed to back each other up. Diana was somewhat jittery at the prospect of spending her summer in a haunted house!

Busying herself with unpacking, she soon forgot the morbid talk and began to feel she would enjoy the pleasant location by the sea. When she'd finished emptying her bags she showered and changed for dinner. Then she slowly made her way downstairs. On the second landing she came face to face with Stefan Emmon. Mavis Norrad's half-brother was one of the company verging on the hippie type. He wore his brown hair long and unkempt, his high forehead dominated a weak, sullen face. Seeing Diana, he frowned uneasily.

She said, "I'm looking forward to rehearsals."

"Wait until you hear what she wants to do to my ballet," Stefan said indignantly. "I don't know whether I can go through with it or not."

Diana frowned. "I think you should listen to Miss Wentworth. She's had so much experience."

"My talent created *Roxanna*," the young man declared indignantly.

"Allow her to polish your work."

"Polish it! She'll change it completely!" he raged.

"Still, I'd listen to her," Diana insisted. "She's old and very wise."

Stefan frowned at her. "I'll tell you what I think. I think her mind is beginning to wander. Ever since she's been here she's been rambling on about this place being filled with phantoms. Even suggesting she is aware of some supernatural presence here."

"She could be right."

"More likely she's senile—or just raving mad," was the young man's disgusted opinion. "I'll go along with her as far as I can. But I make no promises. I may have to withdraw the ballet."

"But you can't do that!" she protested. "We've promised to give low-cost public performances of it in the chapel here in exchange for the free accomodation Mrs. Stoddard is offering us."

"They can use some other ballet if they have to," Stefan said angrily and he walked rapidly down the hall away from her.

She went on to the ground floor. The hallway seemed to be deserted and she moved on rather hesitantly into the luxuriously furnished living room. There she encountered a pretty girl about her own age seated in one of the armchairs, reading a book. Hearing her enter, the girl stood up with a smile.

"You must be one of the ballet company," the girl smiled. "I'm Maggie Evans. I am governess for the children."

Diana returned her smile. "My name is Diana Samson. I am with the ballet and I've only just arrived."

"I'm sure you'll like it here," the pretty girl said. "I'm looking forward to your performances. Miss Wentworth

15

has promised that Carolyn, Mrs. Stoddard's daughter, and I will be able to help with the programs and ushering."

"I'm glad you're interested," Diana said. "It takes a lot of people to operate a theater successfully. And the chapel will be our theater."

"Have you seen it yet?" Maggie asked.

"No."

"It's very old and very quaint. And has some strange and rather eerie legends concerning it."

"Indeed," Diana commented with raised eyebrows. "There seem to be many strange stories about this estate."

Maggie nodded. "I suppose because it is so old. You must meet Mrs. Stoddard's cousin, Barnabas Collins, and have him tell you some of the stories. He makes them seem so real your blood truly chills."

"I'll keep that in mind," Diana said.

"If you'll excuse me, I must begin helping Mrs. Stoddard with dinner," Maggie said, and she left the room.

About a half-hour later dinner was served in the wood-paneled dining room. Candles decorated the table over which Elizabeth and her brother, Roger Collins, presided. Elizabeth mentioned that while the ballet company was in the house the children would eat at a separate table in another room, but the table was still well filled.

Stefan Emmon sat next to Diana and said very little. Mary Wentworth was on her other side. Across the table were Peter Norrad and his young wife Mavis. Diana recalled how jealous the male ballet star was of his pretty, much younger wife, and she felt it would have been better to have seated her half-brother, Stefan, next to her rather than brash, talented Alex Carter.

Alex was in his late twenties and had an arrogant manner. He had talent, but he had come up the hard way from cheap roadshows and showed his background. Handsome in a flashy way, he had shifty eyes.

He smiled across at Diana and said, "Glad you're here at last. So we can get really down to work."

Peter Norrad, his natural enemy, looked at him disdainfully. "I had no idea you were such an enthusiast for work, Alex," he said with sarcasm.

The younger man laughed. "I always enjoy it, especially when I have Mavis working with me."

16

Mavis, an attractive redhead, eyed him demurely. "Thank you, Alex."

Alex reached and took her left hand in his recklessly. This gesture was noted by her husband with anger. For a moment Diana feared there might be a scene at the table. Then Mary Wentworth casually changed the subject and eased the charged atmosphere.

"Are you a lover of ballet, Mr. Collins?" she asked Roger.

Roger Collins scowled. "I've never seen one and I never plan to."

That was that. It punctured all their little vanities and rivalries that this gruff business man had so little interest in them. Diana was anxious to visit the chapel which was to be used as their theater. But by the time she got away from the group it was nearly dark. Remembering the instructions Elizabeth had given earlier, she hurried from the house and found the lane that led to the farmhouse, barns and chapel.

Night shadows closed in around her as she walked quickly along the lane. Within a few minutes she saw the faint outlines of the various buildings against the blue of the night. The chapel, with its peaked roof and bell tower over the entrance, was closest. She saw that it was built of stone, and vines clung to its ancient walls. It seemed to her there was a faint light showing inside it, but she could not be sure.

Then she thought she heard a step in the gravel behind her. Certain that someone was following her, and thinking it might be Alex, or even Stefan, she turned to see who it was. But there was no one! She stood there staring into the darkness for an uneasy moment. She was almost positive she had heard the footstep. Yet she must have been wrong. Unless—and she hesitated at the unnerving thought—unless this had been a manifestation of the spirits everyone at Collinwood had warned her about.

CHAPTER TWO

Diana stood there in the growing darkness with her frightened eyes probing the shadows. A nightbird came winging overhead, seeming to swoop down close to her and then vanishing with a melancholy screeching. She gave a tiny shudder before turning and resuming her walk to the chapel. Now with the night at hand she could clearly see faint light glowing from the chapel's open door and through the stained glass of its windows.

Perhaps fifty yards distant on the right she saw the lighted windows of the farmhouse. That was where the young men and women of the ensemble would be. Her fears suddenly seemed nonsensical and she decided to take a quick look inside the chapel and then go down to the farmhouse and visit for a short while with her friends.

Two worn stone steps led into the chapel. As she stepped inside a feeling of awe came over her. It was a quaint old building with a high vaulted roof and rows of wooden benches with an aisle down the center to what had been the altar. Now the altar had been replaced with a stage on which a nightlight had been set out. It was the glow from this single bare bulb which cast an eerie light through the chapel and which she'd seen outside.

The floor was of slate and she advanced hesitantly along the center aisle towards the stage. A backdrop of a courtyard had been hung in place. She found temporary wooden steps which led to the stage level and went up into the shadows of backstage. From there she moved out onto the stage itself and inspected the floor. It was most important that the stage be solid and the floor smooth for their troupe of dancers. It appeared the carpenters had done their work well.

Again she was filled with apprehension. She had the feeling she was not alone in the silent old building, and, as if to underline her fears, there was a sudden creaking of the floorboards backstage. Swinging around with eyes wide with fear, she gazed into the dark wings, but she could see no one. Yet this time she was positive the sound had been real and not imagined.

She stood there very still, her nerves taut, as she waited for some other warning of danger. Then it came in a way she hadn't expected. A sort of breeze above her head. She quickly glanced up and to her horror saw the gleaming blade of a knife as it came winging through the shadows towards her. She raised her hands in an automatic gesture of self-protection and screamed out in fear.

The knife passed close to her. Wielded by invisible hands it then vanished as abruptly as it had come into view. She stood there dazed, then her eyes wandered to the body of the chapel, and she saw the blurred outlines of a figure standing stock still at the back of the center aisle and regarding her silently.

It was another shock and she gasped out once more. As she did so, the somber figure advanced towards her. In the light from the single bulb, she was able to make out something of the silent bystander. He was a tall man wearing a dark, caped coat and carrying a cane. It took her only a moment to guess that this must be the cousin from England, Barnabas Collins.

"Mr. Collins?" she asked nervously.

The man nodded. "I am Barnabas Collins," he said in a deep, mellow voice.

"I couldn't see you clearly for a moment," she apologized.

"And I fear that I frightened you," Barnabas Collins said coming close to the front of the stage so that she could see him clearly. He had a handsome, rather melancholy face with deep-set burning eyes, a Byronic face. His thick black hair was loosely brushed across his forehead, and his skin had an unusual sallow tint.

Diana was embarrassed at having made herself ridiculous before this self-assured man, and said, "I guess I was determined to see phantoms. But I just had a strange experience."

"Indeed?" the question came in a polite, sonorous voice.

Diana's fear had turned to confusion on being faced by

19

the handsome stranger. She wished she hadn't made such a scene, but she had no choice but to explain. She pointed to the space above the stage.

"I saw a knife up there," she said. "It came swinging towards me as if carried by an invisible hand. Then when it came very close it vanished."

A thin smile played about Barnabas' lips. "That fits in very well with the legend of the chapel. Are you sure you haven't been allowing yourself to listen to such accounts and as a result your imagination got out of control?"

"Oh, no!" she protested. "I saw the knife."

"Propelled by an invisible hand," he said. "Yes, it may be true that you did see such a phenomena."

"Please explain!"

The man standing before the stage gazed up at her wisely. "That could take some time, Miss—" He hesitated at her name.

"Diana," she volunteered quickly. "Diana Samson. I'm with the ballet company."

"Wonderful," he said. "Are you a principal or one of the supporting dancers?"

"I am second lead."

"Then you're probably staying at Collinwood, the main house," he said.

"Yes."

"I'm happy to meet you, Diana," he said. "If you'd care to join me down here perhaps I can satisfy you about the legend."

There was an enormous magnetism about this British cousin of the Collins family. Diana at once left the stage and came down the wooden steps into the main body of the chapel. He bowed, a courtly figure in the caped coat, and, indicating a front bench, invited her to sit down. She did.

Looking up at him, she said, "Maggie Evans mentioned you to me."

He smiled, his perfect white teeth revealed. "I trust she was complimentary."

"Very," she assured him. "And she said you were the one to tell me about the phantoms that stalk Collinwood."

The man in the caped coat stood silhouetted against the stage light. And she couldn't help thinking it no wonder

20

the local people regarded him with uneasy superstition. With his period-style clothing and strange cast of countenance, he might have stepped out of the past.

His burning eyes met hers directly. "Do you believe then that phantoms do exist here?"

She blushed under his direct gaze. "I haven't given it much thought. But it seems everyone has mentioned it. Then as I walked along the lane to the chapel just now I felt I was being followed. When I saw the gleaming blade of the knife hovering over me it was the last straw."

Barnabas Collins smiled faintly. "I can imagine. Mary Wentworth is being very courageous bringing her company here to the chapel. For years it has been deserted as a place with a curse on it."

"I don't suppose she knows," Diana volunteered.

"On the contrary," Barnabas said. "I discussed it with her. But I think the possibility of the place being haunted appeals to her. She is an odd old lady."

"And a very talented one."

Barnabas sat down on the bench beside Diana. "I do not deny that," he said, leaning both hands on the wolf's head cane. "The legend of the chapel began about a hundred years ago. There was a daughter of the household, Anya Collins, who fell in love with a foreign seaman who sailed in one of her father's clipper ships. When they found themselves involved in a romance, the two decided to marry. The young man, Mario Renzie, planned to give up his life as a sailor and find himself a farm in Collinsport. He was a youth with good looks and strength of character, but he had no money. Anya's father was incensed at the idea of the penniless sailor wanting to marry his daughter, and he refused to countenance the match."

Diana smiled at the man. "You make it sound as if you might have actually known them."

He smiled. "The story is very familiar to me. Mario decided to leave the village and seek out an uncle in Boston, whom he felt sure would supply him with the money needed for a small farm. It was the youth's hope that when he had the farm Anya's father would agree to the marriage. He wrote a note to the girl and gave it in the keeping of a sailor friend to get it to her. Then he left on his mission to Boston. Unfortunately the friend to whom

21

he'd entrusted the note went on a drunken spree and lost it. Worse than that he forgot all about it. Poor Anya was left with the conviction that Mario had deserted her without a word."

"What a dreadful thing for her," Diana murmured.

"It was," Barnabas agreed. "In fact it drove her to a desperate act. Her older sister had been recently married and had left her wedding dress at Collinwood. Anya, broken-hearted, found the gown one dark midnight and put it on. Then she came to the chapel on the very date they'd planned for their wedding and hanged herself from a rafter above the altar." He turned and with a nod indicated the stage. "Just over where the stage is now."

Diana gazed up at the spot and recognized it as exactly where she'd had her vision of the gleaming knife blade. "Who found her?"

"Her lover," Barnabas said solemnly. "He arrived back from Boston that very night with the money he needed. Because this chapel had been a favorite rendezvous with them and it was the night when they were supposed to have been married here, he decided to come straight here on the chance Anya might have had the same sentimental idea. You can imagine his excitement as he came hurrying into the darkened chapel to look for his love and tell her the good news. And you can also picture his shock and horror when he saw her shadowy form suspended from the rafter and knew she had taken her own life. He ran from the chapel and then made his way across the fields to the cliffs and threw himself from Widows' Hill. The legend goes that almost as soon as his body was battered on the rocks below the bell in the tower of the chapel began to toll. It wakened the household at Collinwood and Anya's father and others came to see what it meant."

"And found Anya's body," she said.

"Yes," he nodded. "But there was no one in the bell tower. It was as if the bell had been tolled by a phantom. Later Mario's body was found when the tide went out and the legend was born. The superstitious claimed that it was Mario's ghost that had rung the bell and summoned them to find Anya's body. And so the story has come down through the years."

"Did the bell ever ring in a ghostly fashion again?" she asked.

"Yes. Anya's father was found dead in the chapel a few years later. He was seated on one of the rear benches and his face had gone purple and there was a look of fear in his open eyes. Some claimed there were marks on his throat that indicated he'd been strangled by invisible hands. And so the legend of the mysterious ghost was further bolstered. The medical verdict was that he had died of a stroke. He had become melancholy after his daughter's suicide and spent much time sitting in the chapel alone. Also he'd suffered a small stroke prior to this."

Diana stared at Barnabas solemnly. "So it could have been a natural death?"

"It could have," the man seated beside her agreed, but there was a strange expression on his face as he went on. "Still, one thing was difficult to explain. The farmhand that found him insisted he'd gone to the chapel because he'd heard the bell toll. And then again no one was found in the bell tower." He paused significantly. "Over the years the bell is reputed to have tolled more than once to announce the death of someone at Collinwood."

She gasped. "It's a fantastic story," she said. "What do you think of it?"

His smile told her nothing. "More importantly, what do you think of it?" he asked.

"I don't know," she confessed, caught up in the eerie atmosphere of the chapel and the strange story he'd narrated. "But the legend of a mysterious ghost seems to fit with my experience of seeing a knife wielded by an invisible hand."

"That is why I felt I should tell you the story," Barnabas Collins said.

She gave him a worried look. "I don't think I'll come here alone at night again. Ever!"

"Are you so afraid of the supernatural?" Barnabas enquired softly.

Diana hesitated. "It is something I know so little of. Something I don't understand!"

"That is the tragedy," he said. "So few people have a

23

proper knowledge of the world of phantoms."

"You talk as if you do."

"In a modest way. I have made a personal study of the unknown."

She frowned. "If people are so afraid of this place how can we expect to have them come here for the ballet performances?"

"Most of those who attend will be tourists who haven't heard the story," he suggested. "And the others, the locals will come out of curiosity knowing there will be plenty of people here to keep them company. I don't think the legend will hurt your box-office."

"I hope not," she said with a wan smile. "We badly need the money."

"In any case," he said, "it is my belief that the ghost of Mario Renzie would do no more than attempt to frighten you. If his phantom still lurks in the chapel it is to seek revenge from the members of the Collins family still living here."

She gave a tiny shudder. "I'm beginning to believe in it all."

He smiled. "I'll show you the graves of Anya and Mario some time. They are buried in the old cemetery just back of this building. Side by side they have rested there all through the years."

"How stupid of her father not to have allowed them to marry!"

"Such stupidities are much too common and repeated over and over," was his comment.

She stared at him. "You're only a visitor here, yet you seem to know so much about the place."

"I am a Collins," he reminded her, "And I have made a study of the family history."

Diana was thinking quickly, trying to recall what the taxi driver had said about the gaunt, handsome man seated beside her. He'd mentioned his odd clothing and then dwelt on the fact that Barnabas seldom showed himself in the daytime. That he was reputed to walk in the cemetery near the old house at night.

She said, "There is another cemetery on the estate, isn't there?"

"Yes. Near the house I'm occupying," he agreed.

"Many of my near and dear are buried there."

"As a student of history I imagine you dedicate a great part of your days to delving into the past," she said. "Do you work long hours?"

"Yes. I seldom leave my desk during the day," he explained. "Hare, my servant, acts as a barrier between me and interruptions. I wind up my work at sunset each evening. I normally leave the house at dusk. So I shall look forward to your nightly performances."

She smiled. "Are you interested in ballet?"

"In all the arts," he assured her. "I have seen many of the great ballet performances of our time. I know Mary Wentworth to be an accomplished dancer. Now I assume she must be a fine director."

"I feel I'm learning a lot from her," she said.

"We must meet again, Diana," he said, rising. "Don't forget I've promised to show you those graves."

She also got to her feet. "I'm not liable to. Nor am I likely to forget the story you told."

"I merely repeated it as I've heard it," he said.

Diana gave him a searching look. "Have you ever heard the bell in the tower toll?"

His deep-set eyes had a burning glitter. "Yes," he said quietly. "Long ago."

She was about to ask him when and the circumstances surrounding the event when a soft footstep from the back of the chapel caught her attention. Straining, she made out a feminine figure in the aisle. It was Eleanor, a girl in the ensemble with whom she'd struck up a friendship.

Eleanor came up to them with a smile on her pretty face. She was petite and dark. "Miss Wentworth told me you were here," she said.

Diana smiled. "I wonder how she guessed? But I am glad to see you." And she introduced the girl to Barnabas.

Barnabas took the girl's hand in his and with a bow touched his lips to it. "I can see your company has no lack of charm or beauty," he said in his polished fashion.

Eleanor blushed. "I'm sure we do need to develop our talent," she said. "But Miss Wentworth has plans for that."

Barnabas Collins escorted them out into the open again. And true to prediction it was cool outside. He said goodnight and walked off in the direction of Collinwood, a solitary figure in the soft moonlight, as they stood ready to go to the farmhouse to join the company.

Eleanor stared after the tall man in the caped coat as he gradually merged into the darkness. "He seems a very lonely person, doesn't he?" she asked Diana.

Diana sighed. "I'd say so. He's a scholar. I think he devotes a great deal of his time to studying the Collins family history."

The dark girl turned to her with a smile. "A handsome man like that should find many better ways to occupy his time."

"I think he's a bachelor," Diana said. "And he seemed to like you. Better watch out."

"I wouldn't mind getting to know him better," Eleanor said frankly. "But I'd say it was you he's interested in."

"I doubt if he's interested in that way in anybody," Diana retorted quickly. "Some men are born to be bachelors. And they enjoy being alone."

"Somehow your Barnabas Collins doesn't strike me as being the type," the dark girl said.

Accordion music and sounds of revelry came from the lighted farmhouse. When Diana and Eleanor walked the short distance back there they found a party in full swing. A number of the dancers had formed some square dance sets and the dance was going well. Diana joined some of the others in watching from the sidelines.

The company had settled into the farmhouse and were evidently enjoying their visit to this remote part of the country. For most of them it was the first trip to Maine. Diana's thoughts were still filled with memories of Barnabas Collins. She had been uniquely impressed by the tall, stately man. She could not join fully in the merriment for thinking of him. Eleanor had also seemed taken with the gaunt, handsome Barnabas, but in her light-hearted fashion she had now joined one of the square dance sets. The dark, pretty girl went through all the figures with a saucy smile as Diana watched.

In the midst of the revelry the door from outside opened and a haggard-faced Peter Norrad entered and looked around the room with a scowl. Then he moved across to where Diana was standing watching the fun.

Touching her arm the aging male star of the ballet asked, "Have you seen my wife?"

She glanced at him in surprise. "No."

Peter Norrad frowned. "She and Alex Carter left the house together. They said they were coming here."

Diana tensed. She knew that Mavis flirted indecently with the younger male star of the company whenever her husband's back was turned. She hoped there would be no flare-up now when they all needed to work together to save the Mary Wentworth troupe.

She said, "You might have misunderstood them."

Peter Norrad glared at her. "I know what my wife said," he snapped.

"They're not here."

"So I see," he said studying the party-makers grimly. Though he was still a good dancer, he was not popular with the company. Many of the members considered him mean and cruel and did not blame Mavis for being friendly with other men. But Diana felt sorry for the older man and considered Mavis to blame for much of the trouble.

She said, "If I see them I'll tell them you're looking for them."

He gave her an angry glance. "They already know that," he said. And he turned and quickly walked off and out of the farmhouse.

Diana stared after him and began to worry about what could happen. This finally made her slip quietly out of the farm kitchen before the dance had ended. She made her way through the night in the direction of Collinwood.

She'd not gone far before she regretted leaving the farmhouse alone. If she'd asked, any one of the young men there would have been glad to have walked back to the mansion with her. But she'd chosen to go alone and now she was beginning to have fears torment her again.

The moon was not full, but it did provide some light. Ahead she saw the stark outline of Collinwood. And she fervently wished it was much closer. Suppressing her fear as best she could she pushed on until she reached the front lawns of the big house.

There she was confronted with a figure barring her path to the door. She hesitated and then drew a sigh of relief as

27

she saw that it was not some dread phantom but the composer, Stefan Emmon.

Rushing up to him, she asked, "Have you seen Mavis?"

"No," he said sullenly. "Why should I have?"

"I'm trying to find her to warn her," she said. "Her husband was at the farmhouse just now looking for her. Apparently she went off somewhere with Alex Carter and Peter's in a nasty mood."

"Peter is nearly always in a nasty mood," Stefan said.

"We don't want any trouble now that we're about to do your ballet," she pointed out.

"Might be a good thing if we called it off," was his reply. "The way that old crone is changing my work around there won't be anything original of mine left."

"I doubt that," she said.

"Anyway what Mavis does is her own business," the young man said. "I'm not her guardian."

"You are related."

"That doesn't cheer me exactly," he said with sarcasm. "If Peter Norrad can't manage his own wife he needn't expect me to. Mavis and Mary Wentworth between them are garroting my *Roxanna*!"

Diana realized there was little use trying to talk reasonably to the self-centered young composer. She said, "If you should see Mavis warn her about Peter."

"Why should I?" he demanded.

She made no reply. There were times when she felt sure he hated his half-sister. Yet it was Mavis who'd gotten him the position with the ballet troupe and had Mary Wentworth consider his original ballet.

Diana entered the front door of Collinwood and found herself in the dimly lighted hallway, on whose wall the picture of the long-ago Barnabas Collins hung. She stared at the dark oil portrait and was struck by the resemblance the man she'd talked to in the chapel bore to it.

The present Barnabas Collins was indeed a look-alike for his ancestor. The great house was deathly quiet. She slowly made her way up the several flights of stairs to her own room. It wasn't late but she felt weary and ready for bed. Mary Wentworth had scheduled a first rehearsal for the following morning at eleven.

She frowned to herself as she entered her bedroom and closed the door after her. It had been a baffling evening. She'd found the chapel—indeed all of Collinwood—cloaked in an air of eerie mystery. Her meeting with Barnabas Collins had left her with the impression there was some strangeness about him she did not fully understand. He was charming but there was a reserve in his manner she could not explain.

Slowly she undressed and prepared for bed. Almost the minute she turned out the lights and her head touched the pillow she fell asleep. She had no idea how long she remained sleeping, for when she stirred finally to open her eyes it was still pitch dark in her room. And then she realized what had wakened her!

From a distance there came the dismal tolling of a muted bell. Its sad note and the direction from which it came left no doubt in her mind that it was the chapel bell she was hearing. The bell which tolled only at the command of a phantom hand!

For long minutes the bell gave forth its melancholy message. Then it stopped. She lay there in the darkness nervously waiting for it to begin again. But it didn't. She wondered what it signified. Had some of the boys in the company tolled the bell for a prank? Or was it a supernatural warning of the death of a Collins? She pondered these things for some time before eventually drifting off to sleep again.

When she went downstairs the following morning she was surprised to encounter Mary Wentworth in earnest conversation with a frowning Roger Collins. On her approach the two gave her a somewhat guilty glance.

Then Mary came to meet her with a troubled look on her lined, white face. "We have already had a casualty in the company," she said.

Remembering the tolling of the bell an icy fear touched Diana's heart. "What sort of casualty?"

"Your friend Eleanor fell from the cliffs. Fortunately she didn't stumble off a high place and so was not killed. But she was so badly injured she had to be taken to the hospital in Ellsworth. Have you any idea if there was drinking at the party in the farmhouse last night?"

"I don't think so," she said, upset. "Eleanor was with me for quite a long time. I'm certain she couldn't have had much to drink."

Mary looked grim. "We shall have to get on without her," she said. "It should be a lesson to the others."

Roger now spoke up. "I can't imagine her being so careless as to wander where she did. It's a mysterious business."

Diana said, "She couldn't know the cliff path too well. She might easily have become confused and nervous when she lost her footing."

"There is more to it than that," Roger said with a stubborn look. "She's been somewhat incoherent since the accident, but she should be able to give a statement later in the day. When we found her she had a peculiar red mark on her throat."

Diana stared at him. "A peculiar red mark?"

He nodded significantly. "Similar to ones we've seen before on the throats of local girls who've been attacked by some mysterious character and left wandering in hysteria. We haven't been able to get a description of who it is as yet but the local police have tagged him the vampire."

"Why the vampire?" she asked incredulously.

His eyes met hers. "There is a vampire legend associated with Collinwood. And these marks on the girls' throats resemble the teethmarks of a giant bat."

CHAPTER THREE

The revelation came as a shock to Diana. She said, "What sort of vampire legend?"

Roger glanced at his wristwatch. "It's much too long a story for me to go into now. I'm due at my office. Ask Elizabeth. She can tell you." Addressing himself to a pale Mary Wentworth he said, "And my advice to you, Madam, is to warn the young women of your troupe against wandering around alone after dark."

The old woman bowed her head slightly. "Thank you, Mr. Collins. I'll remember that."

The blunt businessman gave them both a resigned look and then left. Diana accompanied Mary into the dining room for breakfast, and she noticed when the white-haired woman helped herself to orange juice her thin, veined hands were trembling.

As they sat down at the table after making a choice from the breakfast buffet set out on the sideboard the old woman glanced at her and said, "I don't like any of this. I'm afraid we may have made a mistake coming here."

Diana was surprised to hear her speak in that manner. "But we would have had to disband the company otherwise," she reminded her.

The pale, wrinkled face of the old woman was concerned. "This is not a happy place. I can sense it. There is a shadow over this house and that poor child Eleanor has been the first to pay the price for us being here."

"It was probably only an accident," Diana protested over her coffee though she was by no means certain in her own mind that it was.

Mary's sharp eyes fixed on her. "There is trouble brewing between Peter and Mavis. He has been patient, but one day he will kill her. And the atmosphere of hatred and tension here is an inviting setting for murder."

"It will never come to that," Diana said. But she

couldn't forget Peter's angry face.

They were soon joined at the table by Mavis and her husband. Peter still looked tense and pale, but he greeted Mary Wentworth warmly enough. The attractive, redhaired Mavis was cool and independent in manner and said little to anyone. When the brash Alex Carter came in to have just coffee he wore a smug smile. Peter ignored him, but Mavis was bold enough to return the ballet star's smile. Mary Wentworth observed this little drama in grim silence.

Diana left the table first and Alex came after her. In the hall he jocularly placed an arm around her as if he were going to kiss her on the cheek. She angrily pushed him away and, opening the front door, went out into the sunshine of the steps and stood looking out at the bay.

Alex followed her and went about lighting a cigarette. His arrogant face showed anger as he asked her, "Why are you so uppity all of a sudden?"

She flashed him a stern look. "You should know after the way you and Mavis carried on last night."

The young man in the dark slacks and cream sport shirt shrugged. "We went for a walk. Any harm in that?"

"Ask her husband."

"Peter is a suspicious idiot. He's jealous of all his wife's friends. And he's jealous of me as a dancer."

Diana gave him a cold smile. "I think that's funny. You can't touch Peter Norrad as a dancer."

"See where we both are in five years," Alex said disdainfully and he took a deep puff on his cigarette.

"You're so selfish you don't care what happens," she accused him. "Your smart tricks could break up the company. And you aren't even aware that Eleanor was hurt last night!"

"Eleanor hurt? How? Where?" he demanded.

She told him, ending with, "You'd have known it if you hadn't been so wrapped up in your own affairs."

He gave her an apologetic smile. "Sorry, Diana. I guess maybe I have been a little out of line. I don't want to cause any trouble. I'll watch my step with Mavis."

She wasn't too impressed. She was familiar with his tactics of making apologies and then going ahead to do the same bad things all over again. She said, "I hope you have intelligence enough to be careful."

32

"I will," he promised, tossing his unfinished cigarette away into the grass. "What about seeing Eleanor?"

"I plan to get a ride up to the hospital when she's well enough to see visitors."

"We can use my car," Alex said with apparent sincerity. "What do you think happened to her? She's not the type to drink too much and stumble over the cliffs."

"I realize that," Diana said. "There's a mystery attached to it and I doubt if it will be solved until we can talk to her." She had been doing a lot of thinking about the red mark of the vampire on her friend's throat but she didn't want to discuss that with Alex. In the first place he wouldn't know what she was talking about. And also, she hadn't enough information on the subject to discuss it intelligently.

She had no chance to question Elizabeth about the series of attacks that had been made on girls in the area of Collinsport. It was soon a few minutes before eleven and time for her to report to the chapel for rehearsal. She made up her mind to talk to Elizabeth about the vampire legend later. She would also mention the subject to Barnabas Collins when she met him again. He seemed to know all the odd facts about the history of the estate. It was likely he could offer her some information on this vampire business as well.

Maggie had asked permission to bring David and Amy along for the rehearsal and Mary Wentworth had said it would be all right. Carolyn had only three-quarters of an hour before she had to report for work at the gift shop in the village. But she went along with Maggie and the children to watch from the rear of the chapel.

Diana strolled along the lane with them. Alex Carter had driven over with Mary Wentworth in his car. She didn't know whether Peter and Mavis would be late or if they had already left. And Stefan Emmon was undoubtedly busy at the chapel. He often ran through new numbers at the piano before the regular rehearsals began.

As Diana and the two girls came within sight of the chapel with David and Amy trailing behind, Carolyn asked her, "What is *Roxanna* about?"

Diana smiled. "It's a kind of fantasy."

Maggie, walking on her other side wanted to know,

33

"And what part do you play in it?"

"I play a friend of Roxanna," Diana said. "And I also understudy for Mavis, who is playing the leading part."

David and Amy had caught up to them by this time and the bright young David asked, "Could you tell us the story of the ballet so we'll be able to follow it?"

Diana said, "Yes, I think so." They had arrived in front of the chapel, and it was quite a busy place with all the dancers and the others assembling. Diana indicated a level area of lawn and suggested, "Suppose we sit down over there for a few minutes and I'll quickly sketch in what the plot of the ballet is."

The four settled down on the grass in a kind of half-moon. Amy was nearest with a solemn look on her young face. "I've studied ballet," she said. "We did a scene from *Giselle* and I was the peasant girl."

Diana smiled. "This ballet takes place in a small village in France and Roxanna is also a peasant girl. It begins at a party with everyone dancing and having a good time. Roxanna is the favorite of everyone and flirts wildly with the young men."

Maggie said, "That's the part Mavis plays."

"Yes," Diana said. "Mavis teases the village youths and is having a wonderful time, when a stranger suddenly arrives at the party. He is such a grim, weird sort of man that all the others stop laughing and dancing and move back from him. But the girl Mavis plays isn't afraid of this unusual intruder."

"Who is the stranger?" David wanted to know.

"That's the mystery," Diana said with a smile. "The part is played by Peter Norrad. He dances with the girl. It is a wild dance and goes on for quite a long while. This is a wonderful scene for Peter and Mavis. Then Peter flings his cloak over her and they dance off into the night and vanish."

"Is that the end of the ballet?" Carolyn asked.

"No," Diana said. "There is a second act. Roxanna returns next morning an old woman. None of her young friends recognize her. They think she is some crazy old crone. Roxanna is desolate. But then the young man who loves her comes along, that part is played by Alex Carter, he at once knows her and takes her in his arms and kisses

34

her. Magically her beauty and youth return. And best of all she has learned not to be a cruel flirt. So the story ends with the entire village dancing in honor of her engagement."

Maggie laughed. "I think it's a fine story."

"Like a fairy tale," Amy ventured.

David looked manly and disgusted. "Fairy tales are for girls!"

"And girls have to go to work," Carolyn said wearily as she got up from the grass. "I don't believe I dare stay any longer, Diana. But I'll come back another time."

"You'll be welcome," Diana assured her. "And you others can find a back seat in the chapel and be very quiet. Miss Wentworth doesn't like any noise in the auditorium when she is directing."

Having given Maggie and the children this advice, Diana went on into the shadowed chapel where Mary Wentworth, seated in one of the front rows, was lecturing to the ensemble gathered onstage. Diana quietly made her way to the murky backstage area to join the other principal players in the ballet and wait for her entrance.

She was waiting quietly when a hand touched her arm and she turned to see Peter Norrad standing by her. He looked stern. "I'm sorry I bothered you about Mavis last night," he said in a low voice. "I was very upset."

"It was all right," she whispered back.

"You have been a good friend to us," he said, "but one should not impose on friendship."

She smiled at him. "I understand."

"Thank you. I see now that I must not involve others in the quarrels we have. It is something that must be settled between ourselves."

Before Diana had any chance to make a reply their cue came to move onstage. A moment later they were all part of the merry party going on in the make-believe world of the ballet. Stefan Emmon labored at the piano and watched them at the same time with an agonized expression on his face.

As Diana moved about in the dance, it occurred to her that this was a very highly strung young man who could actually be on the verge of a breakdown. The company was filled with sensitive talents who might explode in tem-

35

peramental outbursts at any moment. As she danced her
part, her eyes wandered to the dark cavern of the chapel
and she saw the brave, frail figure of Mary Wentworth as
she followed the action. And she thought about Barnabas,
who had made his appearance there last night and introduced himself. Afterward Eleanor had arrived to meet
the handsome stranger through her.

She suddenly was faced with the question of whether
that could have had any bearing on what had happened to
Eleanor later that night. She couldn't believe that it had.
And yet?

"Stop!"

Mary Wentworth's high-pitched voice sounded over the
piano to bring the company to a halt. She came forward to
give them all instructions. "You are very clumsy," she
said impatiently. "Clumping about the stage like awkward
animals."

Diana listened intently. She had to think not only of her
own role but also of the lead played by Mavis. For it was
her responsibility to study the star role and be ready to
substitute in it at the shortest notice. She looked around
her at the young men and women in their dark rehearsal
tights. Some of them were listening intently and others appeared bored.

Mary Wentworth finished correcting them and stepped
back for Stefan Emmon to resume the opening music. The
party scene was gone through once more, and then several
times after that. The old director wanted it to be perfect.

Fortunately the chapel remained cool, because it was
warm outside. The rehearsal continued right through the
luncheon hour. During a break Diana went down to
the rear of the chapel and discovered that Maggie and the
children had left. No doubt bored by the repeated run-
throughs of individual scenes in the ballet. It was tiring
even for the participants, but it was the only way to build
the show into a success.

It was two o'clock before Mary Wentworth dismissed
the company. "We shall rehearse again this evening at
eight," she announced. "We have only ten days before the
ballet opens and we must be ready."

Diana returned to Collinwood for a light lunch. She

phoned the hospital and learned that Eleanor would not be seeing visitors until the next day. This settled, she went to discuss her costume for the ballet with Mary Wentworth.

The old woman was resting on the bed in her room. She listened to Diana's query and told her, "The trunks with the costumes are already at the chapel. I had them placed backstage. Why don't you go over there this afternoon and see what you can find that is suitable? We may have to order additional costumes if we haven't enough."

Diana had planned to rest a little, but she realized the costume problem was a pressing one. It would probably be wise to postpone her rest and see just what kind of condition the costumes were in and how many there were of them.

She said, "Very well. I'll go. Are the trunks locked?"

"Yes," Mary Wentworth said. "The keys are on the ring on my dresser. Take them with you."

Diana found the keys and left for the chapel. It was a hot afternoon with the sun blazing down. She walked quickly along the lane. Not until she reached the ancient stone chapel with its vine-covered walls did she think again of Barnabas Collins and their conversation of the previous evening. He had mentioned a cemetery as being behind the chapel, and she had a sudden desire to investigate it.

Since there was no need to rush into the chapel and examine the costumes, she first walked around the gray edifice to the burial place at its rear. The cemetery had plainly not been in use for many years. It had no fence, and weeds and grass grew plentifully over graves and, in many cases, covered the inscriptions on tilted headstones. More than a few of the gravestones had fallen over completely and some had been broken, possibly by vandals.

Graveyards invariably gave her an odd feeling of being watched and listened to by those long-dead. And this one proved no exception. She moved among the stones and found the grass had grown up in a disgraceful way. Then she was suddenly confronted by a grave that had been partly dug open. It was a shocking surprise in the ancient cemetery, but even more shocking was her discovery that it was the grave of Mario Renzie. His name was still visible in weathered script upon the gray surface of the gravestone!

Her eyes wide with fright, she stood back from the dark earth of the opened grave and wondered what it could mean. Had the phantom literally torn itself from the coffin to stalk the estate and toll the bell in the tower last night? She had mentioned hearing the bell to no one as yet. She'd been waiting to discuss it with Barnabas first, fearing the others would not believe her. At best they would accuse her of being the victim of a nightmare.

She stood there staring at the vandalized grave with horror. The hot sun blazed down and a bee came lazily buzzing by and then went on its way. She was literally transfixed by the implications of her discovery. For she was sure this partly opened grave was in some way linked to the tolling of the tower bell which she'd heard in the small hours of the morning and the mysterious accident which had befallen Eleanor.

Her eyes wandered to the equally weathered stone beside that of Mario Renzie's and she saw that it had the name of Anya Collins on it. Barnabas had been right when he'd told her that they'd been buried side by side— That they had spent all the long years together in death in grim defiance of their being denied the right of being together as man and wife while they lived.

She moved back slowly from the desecrated grave and went around to the entrance to the chapel. She had momentary thoughts of going to the old house where Barnabas was living and asking his servant if she could see him for a few minutes. But she doubted that Barnabas would see her, or even that the servant would deliver her message. Barnabas had been very definite in stating that he resented any disturbance of his studies during the day. She would simply have to somehow control her fears and impatience until the evening.

A rehearsal had been scheduled but would probably not last longer than ten o'clock. If Barnabas came to the chapel while they were still working, she'd explain. She hoped he'd understand and either wait for her or return for her when the rehearsal had ended.

She entered the chapel and again was aware of its almost clammy coolness. Glancing ahead at the stage she was startled by the sight of a shadow which almost made it seem as if a body was hanging there. She thought of how Anya Collins had hung above the altar from a rafter a century ago and that her bones were resting not many feet distant in the grave behind the chapel. It made her halt a moment until the illusion ended and she realized she was allowing her nerves to dominate her.

She went up the temporary wooden steps and pushed through the masking curtains to the shadowed backstage area. It took a moment for her eyes to become accustomed to the near darkness. She fumbled in her pocket for the key ring with the trunk keys. And she debated whether to try to drag the big trunks out to stage center so she could get a reasonably good idea of the costumes packed inside them and their condition.

But the trunks racked against a side wall looked formidably heavy. So she decided to open them where they were and carry the costumes out onto the stage for examination. She inserted the proper key in the first trunk and opened it. It appeared to be only partly-filled with costumes. She reached in and lifted out a full armload to take out to the stage. Afterward she made a second trip and a third until the trunk was empty. Then she moved on to the trunk next to it.

She had just inserted the key in its lock and was swinging the lid back when she heard a slow creaking noise close behind her. It made her freeze with fear and stare straight ahead as she listened. What followed was just as frightening. The air was suddenly filled with the stench of damp earth, earth molding without sunlight. And a vision of that dug-up grave crossed her mind as she had a terrified picture of some grisly creature raised up from the grave and standing behind her ready to seize her the instant she made a move.

To crown her horror, the sound of tortured breathing made itself heard. The hoarse breathing came from directly behind her and she waited tensely, knowing it must be only a matter of seconds before the thing reached out to grasp her.

She debated crying out for help, but somehow could not summon a scream to her lips. She was unable to do anything but wait like a hypnotized rabbit cowered by a swaying cobra. And then the unknown monster struck and she was gripped roughly by the arms from behind and swung to her feet and around.

The spell of horror was broken. She let out a wild cry for help and attempted to fight back. But it was useless, because the thing held her in a merciless grip. Then she was being propelled forward in the murky backstage and all at once the floor seemed to vanish under her. She was going down into a new and more impenetrable darkness. Something banged above her head with a deafening sound and she was crouched alone on hard earth whimpering and sobbing.

For the first dread seconds she believed that in some way she had been transferred into the depths of a grave, that she was far below the earth in the kingdom of the dead. In that lair of grinning outstretched skeletons and dry dust, she had been abandoned. But then she realized that it was something different.

She was in a kind of cellar below the chapel. Someone had seized her and thrust her down through a trap door and left her abject and nerveless on the earthen floor. With that realization she knew her attacker must have been a human. A human who had been hiding in the cellar when she went backstage. Someone she'd caught in a place where he had no right to be and who had taken this violent means to make his escape and safely dispose of her.

She attempted to stand, but was forced to remain partly crouched as she tried to find the trap door and lift it up. As she groped in the darkness she heard footsteps on the stage above her. In spite of the fetid airlessness of the cellar she found the strength to scream out for help. And she risked injury by pounding her clenched fists against the wood of the floor above her. It brought results. Within a few seconds the trap door was swung open. She had not been far from it—only a few feet to the left. Now she scrambled forward and reached up to try and drag herself to freedom.

Someone helped her, and as she was brought gasping safely on the backstage floor, demanded, "What were you doing down there?"

She stared up in utter dejection to see Stefan Emmon. She gave a small cry of despair. "Do you think I wanted to be in that verminous cellar?"

The young man with the long hair and sullen features glanced down into the dark, moldy opening. "How did you get there?"

"Somebody attacked me and put me down there!" she said angrily.

Stefan lowered the trap door closed. Then he turned to her again. "Did you see who it was?"

She had struggled to her feet in tearful annoyance. "Of course I didn't! It could have been anyone! It could have been you!"

The young composer frowned. "Don't involve me just because I was foolish enough to rescue you."

"I suppose you're sorry you did!"

He eyed her disgustedly. "I'm not getting much thanks."

"I'm sorry," she said, drying her eyes with a hankie. "I'm a little hysterical."

"And what are all those costumes doing dumped out on the stage?"

"That's why I came here. To examine them and see what we'll need extra."

Stefan looked bleak. "You didn't make much headway."

"There's some crazy man loose here," she said indignantly. "That must have been what happened to Eleanor. She was attacked and pushed over the cliff."

"That's no more than a wild guess," he warned her.

"Something like that must have happened," she insisted.

A strange look had come to his pale face. "What about the weird mark I hear she had on her throat? I hear other girls in the area have been attacked in the same way."

"I don't know anything about that."

His smile was malevolent. "I'd guess there are a lot of things you don't know about," he said. "You better watch out. The gossip around the village is that there's a vampire loose at Collinwood."

"That's insane," she declared. She had no desire to take him into her confidence. She would wait until she talked with Barnabas before discussing last night with anyone.

41

Stefan eyed her strangely. "Did it ever strike you that the vampire might be one of us?"

"One of us?"

"Why not?" he asked. "We're a weird enough lot. Suppose one of us is a human touched by the vampire curse. None of the others would guess it until it was too late. Whoever it was could silence them by finishing them off one by one."

She studied the almost insane smile on the face of the young composer and saw that he was enjoying going over the horrifying possibility, and relishing this moment of tormenting her.

She said, "That's a frightening thought."

His manner changed at once. "It's not liable to be true. But I was just trying to prove that nightmare and reality aren't all that far apart."

"You managed very well," she said in a dull voice. The quick sequence of upsetting events had wearied and stunned her.

"Do you want me to help you go over the costumes?" he asked.

"If you like," she said.

The sorting of the costumes took about two hours. Diana became so engrossed in her task that she temporarily forgot the terrifying experience she'd endured. Stefan had proved a good assistant, and by the time they'd finished they knew exactly what they had to work with.

"We'll have to put these back in the trunks," she said, rising.

He nodded. "We'll need at least four new costumes for the principals and a dozen or so for the girls in the ensemble." He eyed the heap of worn costumes on the stage with disgust. "It's like Mary Wentworth to dig up trunks full of junk like this to launch my new ballet."

"She hasn't the money for all new costumes," Diana pointed out.

The composer frowned. "Well, she'll have to order a few. Even if she has to charge them."

"I think she'll be willing to do that," Diana said. "If only all this ghost and vampire talk doesn't scare people away from the performances we can soon earn enough to pay our debts."

Stefan looked skeptical. "We might have known there was a catch to it when that Stoddard woman offered us everything free."

Still grumbling, he helped her take the costumes backstage once more and pack them in the trunks. By the time they'd finished it was time to return to the house for dinner. They left the chapel and started back along the lane in the direction of Collinwood. The sun had vanished, leaving it a cloudy late afternoon. Diana was in a mood as somber as the dark day.

"You going to mention what happened backstage?" Stefan asked her.

"I suppose that would be sensible," she said with annoyance. "I should have reported it right away."

"Good thing I was there or they probably wouldn't believe your story," he pointed out.

"I still have no idea who it was or why he did it," she said.

"Could be somebody who hates ballet dancers," he suggested. "I know I do."

She was about to make a suitably tart reply to that when something stopped her. They had been passing a distant area of thick bushes. And as her eyes casually wandered to the row of bushes she was startled to see a face emerge from them and glower at her. It was a coarse face of criminal expression, and the hatred its owner directed at her was so intense that she halted and cried out.

CHAPTER FOUR

Stefan stopped and stared at her impatiently. "What is it now?" he demanded.

"A horrible face over there in the bushes," she exclaimed and pointed to the spot where she'd seen the scowling stranger.

"I don't see anyone."

He was right. The face had vanished as suddenly as it had appeared. Diana stood there bewildered. "I'm sure I saw it."

His glance was skeptical. "It seems to me you're having more than your share of weird experiences," he told her.

She frowned at him. "You don't believe me?"

"I didn't see the face."

"I still say it was there," she insisted, her own face grim at the memory of that glare of hatred.

Stefan shrugged. "You'd better include that when you talk to the Collins family about what's gone on today."

Diana made up her mind that she would, and as soon as they returned to Collinwood, she sought out Elizabeth Stoddard in the kitchen of the great house. When she gave the pleasant matron a brief account of what had taken place, she noted the growing tension reflected on her attractive face.

When Diana had finished her story, Elizabeth said, "This is frightening and very serious. As soon as my brother returns from the factory I want you to tell him the details again."

So it was that Diana found herself in the book-lined study of Collinwood with Elizabeth and Roger as her audience as she gave a full version of her terrifying afternoon. When she ended with the mention of the coarse face that had glared at her from the bushes, she noticed a meaningful look pass between Roger and his sister.

Roger, standing by his desk, gave her a searching glance.

"Can you give us a more exact description of this face you saw?"

Diana, seated in one of the room's easy chairs, frowned as she attempted to recall clearly the face she'd seen for such a brief moment. Yet it had made such an impact on her it was not too difficult. Slowly she said, "It was what I'd call a criminal face. Coarse and squarish. The eyes were small but evil, and his hair came down on his forehead. He had a low forehead. And I'd suppose he was a large man and very powerful."

From her chair beside Diana, Elizabeth said, "Hank!"

Roger Collins nodded in agreement with his sister. "Just what I've been thinking." And he told Diana, "A few weeks ago a hulking transient came here and asked for work. He offered to hire out at very reasonable wages and claimed he was a good gardener. Matt Morgan has been complaining about having too many chores, so I decided to give the stranger work."

"Which turned out to be a dreadful mistake," Elizabeth said.

"We soon discovered that," Roger Collins went on. "This fellow, whose name was Hank Sheldon, or at least that's the name he gave us, did very little work. On top of this he went to the village every night and came back drunk and ugly."

Elizabeth leaned forward in her chair and told Diana, "He actually started a fight with Matt and we had to discharge him. Since then Matt claims he's been lurking around the estate. We've had an idea he's hiding in one of the outbuildings and your story suggests we've been right."

"He's probably using one of the barns for shelter," Roger said, "and getting his food at one of the farmhouses or in the village. But why he is lingering on here is a mystery I can't explain."

Diana said, "Probably he'd been staying in the chapel until the company came and took it over."

"It's a possibility," Roger agreed. "And he may have left something in the cellar there and gone back to get it. You surprised him and he hid there until a suitable moment then he pounced on you and reversed the situation by making you a prisoner in the cellar. Later he watched

45

from the bushes as you came back here."

"It seems a reasonable explanation," Diana agreed.

"But what can he want here?" Elizabeth worried.

Her brother shrugged. "It could be simply that he's hiding from the police. I've asked the police chief at Ellsworth to try to find out if he's wanted. But it's rather hard to be sure when we have no photograph of him. At any rate, he's still on the property."

"He likely wants to rob or murder us," Elizabeth said with a sigh.

"I doubt it," Roger said dryly. "I certainly hope not. I'll report what Miss Samson has told us to the authorities and perhaps they'll take more interest in the situation. So far I feel they haven't done much."

Diana recalled the vandalized grave and asked, "What would this Hank have to do with the grave I found partly dug up?"

Roger frowned. "I can't see that he'd have anything to do with that. It could be the work of youngsters with nothing better to occupy them. We have some serious vandalism perpetrated occasionally by some of the summer young people."

Elizabeth nodded. "It has to be something like that. It's such a senseless crime."

Diana smiled faintly. "I'm sorry to bother you with all this, but I felt I should."

"You've done right," Roger said brusquely. "I guess you know I wasn't in favor of your company coming here. It was Elizabeth's idea. But since you are here I want you to have protection."

"Thank you," she said quietly. "There have been so many ugly stories of ghosts and such things on the estate that I was beginning to think it had something to do with the supernatural."

Roger regarded her coldly. "You would do well to avoid listening to such idle gossip."

Elizabeth smiled at her uneasily. "All this vampire talk dates back to something that happened nearly two centuries ago. The villagers have long memories. And the story of this mysterious ghost and the tolling of the chapel bell by him is utter fantasy."

It took all the self-control Diana had not to burst out with the news that she had heard the bell the night before. But she was confident if she made such a statement on top of all the rest she'd told them they would put her down as a crank, an irresponsible person who indulged in fantasies. So she kept quiet.

Elizabeth rose from her chair. "Well, I hope nothing more happens," she said.

"I hope not," Diana agreed as she also got up. She saw that the interview was at an end.

Dinner was a quiet affair that night. But just before they left for the rehearsal at the chapel Mavis Norrad singled her out in the living room. In a low voice that could not be heard by the others, the redhead accused her of attempting to cause her trouble.

"Why are you telling my husband stories about me?" Mavis demanded.

Diana had not expected the attack. She stared at the ballet star. "You're very wrong. I've said nothing about you."

"Don't lie!" Mavis said. "I know you'd like to have my part in the ballet and you're trying to get it by turning my husband against me."

"It's not true!"

"Keep away from Peter!" Mavis warned her. "Just remember that." And she left her to join the others at the opposite end of the big room.

Diana was hurt and shocked by the viciousness of the pretty redhead's manner. Of course, it was typical of the temperamental Mavis to blame others for the problems she created for herself.

Everyone arrived at the chapel in time for the eight o'clock rehearsal. Diana had a brief conversation with Mary Wentworth about the costumes and the old woman agreed to send to New York for the additional ones required. Then she sat down in the front row to continue her direction of the ballet.

It was a warm, humid night for Maine, and the strenuous dancing was doubly difficult. But Mary Wentworth was a dedicated choreographer and kept making both ensemble and principals repeat scenes. The time passed quickly. It was almost nine when Mavis and Peter Norrad began the fantastic dance to the lilting tune which Diana was always to recall when she thought of Maine and that summer.

Stefan played the melodic theme with loving care as the two expert dancers created a whirling, swooping poem in motion. Their cleverly executed movements translated the beauty of the music into a graceful tribute to the human form. Diana was not in that particular section of the ballet, so she stood watching from the rear of the darkened chapel.

Mary Wentworth had not interrupted the husband and wife team once, which indicated she felt they were getting everything possible from the sequence. Watching the duo work so beautifully together, Diana mourned that their personal lives could not be so happy and well-balanced. And she also doubted that she could possibly match the artistry of Mavis if she were called on to take over the part.

"A tired performance," a familiar voice said beside her. "He's showing his age."

She turned to see a sneering Alex Carter beside her. In spite of his flashy good looks she found the young man basically cheap and mean. She said, "You could never do as well."

"Don't you believe it," he told her. "I'll be a star when he won't be able to find work."

"Peter Norrad has a quality and style you'll never match," she flared in a low voice, angered by his arrogance.

Alex laughed. "Mavis doesn't seem to agree."

"Wife stealing is the kind of cheap trick you're best at," she told him.

"If you'd take more interest in me I might leave some of the wives alone," he suggested as he attempted to put an arm around her.

"Stop that!' she said angrily and left him to rush out into the cool darkness.

The boldness of the unpleasant Alex Carter had nauseated her. Because of his good looks, he felt he could attract any of the females in the company. His success with Mavis had encouraged this. But Mavis, despite being

48

a fine dancer, could not see through the shallow young man.

Mary Wentworth also was too much impressed by him. One of the reasons being that he had suggested coming to Collinwood for this summer season. He had heard somewhere about the empty chapel and contacted Elizabeth Stoddard. On learning of the company's financial problems she had given them much more than the mere use of the old building. His success in this had won him new respect from Mary Wentworth. Diana greatly doubted that he deserved it.

She felt it had been merely a case of luck. He'd somehow happened to hear about the chapel in the small Maine town and followed it up from there. Now he was doing all he could to cause dissension in the company. She couldn't understand why Mary Wentworth wasn't aware of this, but the old woman was using all her energy to make the ballet a success and noticed little else that went on around her.

With a sigh Diana strolled away from the chapel a short distance. From inside she heard Stefan playing the lilting strains of his beautiful waltz. It meant that Mavis and Peter Norrad were going through their dance once more and that would take the balance of the rehearsal time. She would not be needed again tonight.

A tall figure loomed in the shadows before her, and she at once recognized Barnabas Collins by his cape and the cane he invariably carried. She waited for him to come close.

"Good evening," he said with a courtly bow. "What a lovely waltz tune that is. Usually all the music in ballet isn't that melodic."

"Stefan is a fine composer," she agreed. "Though he is an erratic person. He behaves so moodily that at times I feel he may be a mild mental case."

Barnabas nodded. "Genuis is often eccentric," he said. "So you must be ready to forgive him."

"I find it easier in his case than I do in some others," she said with a touch of bitterness.

Barnabas looked at her in surprise. "You make it sound as if someone in the company is annoying you."

"We do have a trouble-maker," she admitted. "His

49

name is Alex Carter. But I'd rather not talk about him."

"Quite understandable. Do you have to return to the chapel and the rehearsal?"

"No," she said. "They won't need me again. Can we take a stroll somewhere. I have a great deal to tell you. Some strange things have happened since we met last night."

"It's a warm night," Barnabas said. "Would you like to walk as far as Widows' Hill?"

She considered. "That's the very high place on the cliffs. There's a bench there, if I remember correctly."

"There is."

She smiled at him wanly. "And doesn't it have some ghostly legend associated with it also?"

"Yes. It was on Widows' Hill the wives of the fishermen gathered to watch and wait for their husbands to return in their boats. And if the Phantom Mariner showed himself on the hill it meant that one or more of the men had been drowned."

She shivered. "All these stories are so eerie. Do you really believe it to be true?"

"I suppose there must be some basis in fact. But over the years there is a tendency for folk to exaggerate."

"If all the ghost stories one hears are true, Collinwood must be the most haunted of mansions."

Barnabas laughed softly. "You should only accept a small part of what you hear."

"But Widows' Hill has attracted suicides," she recalled. "Some of the Collins family have taken their lives there."

His manner changed at once and the handsome face in the shadows became solemn. "Yes," he said. "Some of them have."

"I'd still like to go there," she said, glancing back at the chapel where the music had ended and the rehearsal would be breaking up. "I want to get away from them while we talk."

They walked swiftly through the dark night in an effort to be well ahead of the others. Diana knew none of them would venture as far as Widows' Hill, so she and Barnabas would have privacy there. They went by Collinwood's lighted windows and she said little. She wanted to save her news for the time when they'd be sitting relaxed on the cliff.

Barnabas gave her a feeling of security even though he had an air about him she did not understand. It was good being with him and she felt he might be able to offer her some helpful advice. In the short time she'd known the cultured stranger she'd come to look on him as a friend.

He gave her a side glance. "You seem secretive and unhappy tonight."

"You're very perceptive," she told him.

"I meant to come earlier," he said. "But my servant did not wake me as usual. I sometimes take a short nap before going out in the evenings."

They came to Widows' Hill at last. And they stood there in silence a moment studying the distant lighthouse on the right, the twinkling points of light that marked the village of Collinsport on the left and the red glow of the marking buoys far out on the bay for pleasure craft. It was dark without any moon, and only a few scattered stars showing overhead.

At last she turned and sat down on the bench. "I hardly know where to begin," she said.

There was a moment of silence between them as he stood staring down at her. The waves washed on the beach below in their melancholy way before he spoke. "I'm waiting," he said.

She gave him a troubled glance. "You remember meeting Eleanor last night?"

"Yes. An unusually attractive girl."

"Something awful happened to her. She stumbled over the cliffs, or somebody shoved her off them. We don't know yet. She was nearly killed. She's in the hospital now. I hope to see her tomorrow."

Barnabas gasped and sat down beside her. "Are you certain of this?"

"Yes." She stared through the darkness at his gaunt, handsome face. "And there's something else."

"What?" he asked, almost sharply.

"There was a red mark on her throat. I understand it's known around here as the vampire's mark. They say that several of the local girls have been attacked by someone

51

this way and left wandering in a kind of daze. They think that whoever put that mark on her throat may have been responsible for pushing her off the cliffs."

"I can't believe that," Barnabas said in a taut voice.

She stared at him. "Why not?"

He hesitated. Then making an awkward gesture he told her, "It never happened before. I mean, none of those other girls suffered that kind of murder attempt. I'd say this was the work of someone else."

"But the mark on her throat was supposedly identical with the others."

"It may have been a coincidence," Barnabas said wearily. "I'm very upset about Eleanor."

"I'll tell her when I see her tomorrow," she promised.

"Please do that," he said.

"Could it have been the mysterious ghost that was responsible for what happened to her?" Diana asked.

The hypnotic eyes of the handsome man seemed to shine in the dark. They fixed directly on hers as he softly asked, "What makes you think that?"

"I woke up in the middle of the night and heard the chapel bell tolling. It must have been about the time the attack was made on Eleanor. And isn't it Mario Renzie's ghost that tolls the bell and seeks revenge on the Collins family?"

"Eleanor was not a Collins."

"But she was staying here. And the bell tolls to signify a death. It was only luck she wasn't killed."

Barnabas sighed and rested his hands on his cane. "Are you sure you didn't have a nightmare and dream that you heard the chapel bell?"

"I was afraid you might think that."

"It's possible. Dreams can be vivid."

"No," she said emphatically. "I did awaken and I did hear that bell."

"I see," he said.

"I kept thinking about it," Diana went on. "But I didn't tell anyone. I wanted to wait and hear what you might make of it."

The man beside her touched his hand on hers and she was surprised that it felt icy cold. It almost sent a shiver

52

through her, but she pretended not to notice. It was likely he had a circulatory problem and might be sensitive concerning the condition.

Barnabas said, "I appreciate the confidence you're showing in me."

She smiled at him. "I knew from the moment we met that I would like you. You are a very unusual person."

His returning smile had a melancholy tinge. "Again may I say that you are most perceptive."

"When I went to the chapel this afternoon to sort out costumes I stopped by the old cemetery to look up the graves of Anya and Mario."

"Yes. I've been intending to show them to you."

She gave him a significant look. "I found them on my own. And the grave of Mario had been disturbed. Dug up, in fact. Someone had vandalized the grave."

"Are you sure it was Mario's grave?" he asked with a hint of tenseness in his voice.

"Yes. I read the gravestone." She paused. Then very carefully she put the question to him, "Was the earth upturned by vandals, or could it have been caused by his vengeful spirit escaping from the coffin?"

He did not reply at once. Then he said, "I see that for you the mysterious ghost really exists."

"I'm sure of it," she said earnestly. "Don't you agree?"

"Until now I was doubtful," he said. "I agree Mario haunted Collinwood at one time. But I felt his spirit had at last come to rest as most unhappy spirits eventually do. Now you make me wonder."

"I'm sure Mario's ghost is on the prowl again," she insisted. "And that he still seeks revenge for himself and Anya."

He smiled sadly. "What a little romantic you are."

"You know all about the history of Collinwood. You are steeped in its traditions. You should be more ready to believe it than me."

"Perhaps."

"Or have you become so befuddled by those dusty volumes you read all day that you have lost your feeling for the estate?"

"Never that," he assured her. "I do take a special interest in the haunting of these acres. And if the ghost has resumed his mischief then we must try to find a way to stop him."

"Would he be part of this vampire legend?" she asked earnestly. "I have never heard the full facts."

"Indeed?"

"No."

He laughed dryly. "If you had, perhaps you would hesitate to be out here in the dark and alone with me."

She frowned. "Why do you say that?"

"The legend of the vampire dates back to my ancestor, Barnabas Collins, the much-maligned man whose portrait you have seen in the hallway of Collinwood."

"Yes. You resemble him to a startling degree."

"So I have been told. About a hundred-and-seventy-five years ago Barnabas Collins was accused of being a vampire and attacking females of the village. The feeling against him became so strong he was forced to flee to England."

"But are there such things as vampires?"

He smiled. "I'm a poor one to ask. What I mean is, I have very decided opinions on the matter. The walking dead, as vampires are termed, do turn up in various historical accounts."

She searched his gaunt face with its deep-set eyes. "Then you do think they exist?"

"Yes. I have reason to believe they exist."

"But this talk about your ancestor being one and still haunting the estate today is utter nonsense."

"I'm glad you think so."

"How did such rumors start?"

"Because of my return," he said almost casually.

She stared at him. "Because of you?"

"Yes. I dress in an out-moded fashion. These village folk do not understand that. They think my habits of work and recreation are strange. Because I do not leave my house until sunset, they choose to see me as a sinister character."

"But you have a perfect right to be individual," she protested. "Many of the men in our company dress as differently as you. And wear their hair as long or longer. Yet no one thinks anything of it."

"Because they are identified with your company," he said. "But no one knows anything about my background or why I am here. They cannot imagine anyone devoting their days to historical study. And then when a few hysterical girls insist they have been attacked by a mysterious stranger the villagers at once think of me. It's only a step from that to link me with my ancestor of the same name and to link him with the walking dead."

"But that's so unfair!"

"I'm glad you feel that way," Barnabas said. "The marks on these girls' throats have apparently done them no harm. They may have been self-inflicted. Some young women like to attract attention to themselves. And how better to do it than announce you've been the victim of a vampire."

She frowned. "Yet, Eleanor had such a mark on her throat when she was found. And I know she wouldn't pretend anything like that."

A strange expression crossed the handsome face. "I have told you that I believe Eleanor's case is an exception. She could have marked her throat when she fell. And her stumbling from the cliff could have come about as the result of some very live human attacking her rather than a ghost."

Diana nodded with excitement. "I'm certain you're right about that. There is some criminal character lurking on the estate. I had trouble with him this afternoon." And she proceeded to tell him about it.

At the end of her story Barnabas said, "You must be careful about wandering around the grounds alone. Even in daytime it won't be safe until they catch this fellow."

"Roger is going to speak to the police again," she said.

He sighed. "I wouldn't count on too much action from them. It's a good deal easier to blame such happenings on a ghost or vampire."

"I agree," she said. "And I can see how such foolish stories start." She smiled at him fondly. "I'm so sorry for you, Barnabas."

His burning eyes met hers. "The marvelous thing is that you sincerely mean that," he said in a hushed voice.

"Of course I mean it!"

"You're a very lovely girl, Diana," Barnabas said. "I

55

have become fond of you in this short time we've known each other. And I fear for you. You shouldn't have come here. You may be in great danger."

"Why do you say that?"

He shrugged. "Call it a sixth sense on my part. Why don't you give up your part in the ballet and leave?"

"I couldn't do that," she said. "It wouldn't be fair to the others. And I believe Stefan's ballet is going to be a success. I'd like to share that success."

"Take care then, my dear," Barnabas said gently. And he took her in his arms for a long kiss. It was a moment she'd been waiting for and it brought her a tremendous feeling of happiness. In his arms she felt secure in spite of all that had happened. And then, very gradually, she became aware of the coldness of his lips. They were even more icy than his hands. And the moment of bliss was shadowed by feelings of apprehension. What did this strangeness about him mean?

A night bird came swooping by almost over their heads and uttered a series of mournful cries. Barnabas at once let her go and stared at her sadly.

CHAPTER FIVE

Diana smiled ruefully. "My nerves must be getting very bad. The cry of that night bird just now sent a chill through me. Everything seems suddenly so strange."

Barnabas was staring at her. "I shouldn't have kissed you."

She touched his arm. "I wanted you to," she said gently. "It wasn't that. I felt odd even before then. And when you kissed me I imagined your lips to be weirdly cold."

"They sometimes are," he said. "My health is not quite normal."

Concern showed in her eyes. "You're not ill?"

"Not really ill," he assured her. "Rather a chronic condition. But nothing that should worry you." He turned to gaze out at the ocean and she had a chance to study his fine profile. "I must admit I'm very fond of you. But I have no right to be."

"You have the right of any man," she told him.

He looked at her again with a melancholy smile. "I'm very lonely and you are a delightful child. But I must be fair to you."

Diana moved close to him and touched her head against his shoulder. In a small voice, she confided, "I'm very fond of you, Barnabas. Perhaps I'm even in love with you."

His arm went around her and the cold lips touched her forehead again. He said, "Now I must see you safely home."

At the door of Collinwood he stood with her. "Are you sure you won't consider leaving the company and getting away from Collinwood before something worse happens to you?"

"I can't leave," she told him. "Mary is counting on me for the ballet, and anyway, I've only just met you."

Barnabas sighed. "Then, at least be extremely careful."

"When will I see you again?"

He hesitated. "Tomorrow night. I'll come by the chapel."

"It seems so long," she mourned. "Can't we ever meet in the daytime?"

"It's extremely unlikely," he said. "I'm sorry."

"So am I," she said. They kissed again and she went inside.

In the privacy of her own room she reviewed the events of the day and night. And she was left more convinced than ever that the isolated estate of Collinwood must truly be haunted. She was even willing to believe that it had not been the transient Hank, the burly worker discharged by Roger Collins, who had seized her and thrust her in the darkness of the cellar beneath the chapel but the spirit of Mario, the mysterious ghost!

Barnabas seemed to believe in the invisible ghost, though he'd not given her any new information concerning the hauntings. He'd also been bitter and withdrawn in discussing the vampire who was supposed to roam Collinwood in the hours of night. No doubt it was because his ancestor's good name had been tarnished by the legend. She was anxious to see Eleanor and question her about her experiences the night she'd stumbled off the cliff. She had the feeling the dark-haired girl might be able to help her.

Her own mood was strange. She knew she was falling in love with Barnabas. A man whom she'd met on only a few occasions and whom she didn't pretend to understand. Yet, love did not always require understanding, and in the handsome, quiet Englishman she'd discovered an ideal. She did not want to be separated from him at this point.

This was the chief reason for her continuing on with the ballet company. Even though Collinwood might hold danger for her, she would not leave. Perhaps Barnabas might soon declare his love for her and they might leave together. It was only a hope. He was very set in his ways as a recluse and a scholar, but it could come about, so meanwhile she was busy with her role in the ballet.

The following morning it was foggy with a wet drizzle. Mary Wentworth sent down word from her room that she was feeling unwell and rehearsals would be postponed until the afternoon. Diana was pleased by this word and made up her mind to hurry to Ellsworth and visit Eleanor in the hospital there. Not all the people in the company had cars and there were some she'd prefer not to travel with, such as Alex Carter.

Then she recalled that Stefan had a small black sedan. Seeking out the aloof young man in the study where he was working on some music sheets, she asked him if he would drive her to the hospital and somewhat nervously awaited his reply.

He looked up from the desk with a slight frown. "When can you be ready?"

"As soon as you like."

"I'll be finished here in another ten minutes," he told her. "I'll take you then. Meet me around at the back where I'm parked."

"Thank you," she said, delighted that it had turned out so well.

He gave her a thoughtful glance. "It's all right," he said and returned to his orchestrations.

She left him feeling much better. In many ways she liked Stefan and considered him a genius, but he could display the eccentricity of genius when he liked. He could be impatient, bad-tempered and sullen. But perhaps as he gained recognition and success in his chosen field his disposition would improve. It seemed this might be likely.

Hurrying upstairs, she found her raincoat and put it on. She also tied a kerchief over her yellow hair. Then she started down to wait for Stefan. On the way she met Elizabeth Stoddard on the second landing.

The dark woman paused to give her a questioning look. "You were with my cousin Barnabas last night?" the mistress of Collinwood observed.

Somewhat surprised Diana said, "Yes, that's so."

"I happened to look out my window and saw you on the steps."

"Oh!" Diana felt her cheeks warm.

"I don't want to interfere in any way," Elizabeth went on quickly. "But I feel I should warn you Barnabas is a wanderer. Not a man to establish strong personal relationships."

59

"I hadn't thought about that," she said quietly.

"I wouldn't blame you if you had," Elizabeth said with meaning in her tone. "Barnabas is charming."

"Yes." She could certainly agree with that.

"But he is not popular in the village. They regard him with suspicion because he is different."

"I know."

"He has visited us before and he always leaves abruptly when you least expect him to. I wouldn't want you to be hurt."

"Thank you," she said.

"Just so long as you understand," the dark-haired woman told her. And then she went on along the corridor.

Diana continued downstairs in a rather stunned mood. Elizabeth's attitude had been hard to understand. She had almost warned her against falling in love with Barnabas, but she had offered no strong reasons for her warning beyond stating that Barnabas was liable to leave suddenly. But Diana thought he mightn't if a true romance developed.

She wished she knew more about the handsome, melancholy man and his immediate past. It seemed unreasonable that he had not married over the years. And yet he appeared to be very much on his own. Still he had shown a hesitance in taking her in his arms and saying that he loved her. He'd seemed to be fighting against the affection he felt for her. Why?

Surely he didn't group her with the ignorant and suspicious villagers. She wasn't the sort of person to dub him a monster because he chose to work during the days and wander for relaxation after dusk came. His way of dressing didn't bother her. In fact, she thought it suited him. She only wished he had more confidence in her ability to understand and love him.

Her reverie was ended by Stefan's arrival. He gave her an impatient look. "I told you I'd be waiting by my car at the back door."

She smiled an apology. "Sorry, I was just going to meet you."

"I hurried so I'd be ready in time," he grumbled as he led her down the long corridor to the rear door.

It was still foggy and wet as she went outside and took

her place in the front seat of the car. The young composer sat behind the wheel and started the motor. In a moment they were on their way out the drive to the uneven and winding road.

He asked, "Do you expect Eleanor will be able to see you?"

"The doctor said she would."

He frowned at the road. "Crazy kind of thing that happened to her."

"Yes."

"This is a mad kind of place," he went on. "My bet is there'll be more trouble before we finish here."

She gave a resigned sigh. "Everyone seemes to take that for granted. And I hope you may all be wrong."

Stefan gave her a sardonic smile. "You underestimate the dire influence of the evil spirits lurking at Collinwood."

"I think most of that talk is nonsense."

"Mary Wentworth doesn't," he assured her. "She says when she was alone in the chapel the other night a glowing yellow globe floated across the stage. She puts it down to some ghost."

"Or her vivid imagination," Diana suggested.

"There is a legend of a mysterious ghost," Stefan insisted. "Maybe he was responsible for what happened to Eleanor."

"I doubt it," Diana said, but she wasn't all that sure. She could still remember that first night on the stage in the chapel when that knife had come swirling through the air close to her head. That knife had seemed real enough, though Barnabas had wondered if she hadn't been frightened by some illusion of lights. She was inclined to think not. Surely a ghostly hand had piloted that knife which had vanished so suddenly. And if so, couldn't the same unseen hand have been responsible for the guidance of the weird yellow globe which Mary Wentworth had said she'd seen.

Stefan must have read the doubt in her silence for he said, "I guess you've been aware of the atmosphere of the supernatural at Collinwood just the same as the rest of us."

"I'm worried more about the ballet and its success," she

61

said. "And so should you be."

He smiled wryly as he kept busy at the wheel, the visibility was poor because of the fog. "I've staked just about everything on *Roxanna*," he admitted. "And I guess Mary Wentworth is beginning to make it come alive."

"I'm glad you finally admit that."

He laughed quietly. "You're like the rest of the company. You don't like me. Not even my half-sister, Mavis, has any real liking for me."

"Not true," Diana said. "We respect you, but we don't know how to get along with you. You seem to enjoy being difficult."

Stefan's eyes were fastened on the fog-ridden road. "No one enjoys being difficult," he said. "I get hung up on my music sometimes. Composing isn't all that easy."

"I'm sure it isn't," she admitted.

"People like me live a kind of double life," he said. "A lot of the time when you put me down as unfriendly I'm merely trying to work out some difficult theme in my head."

"I'll grant you that," she said. "It's still hard to get through to you. Or feel a warm friendship for you."

He gave her a bitter glance. "Do you hate me?"

It was her turn to smile incredulously. "Certainly not!"

"You've never made an effort to be friendly with me," Stefan went on in his serious way. "Yet I rescued you yesterday afternoon and I've always tried to show I like you. Driving you to Ellsworth now is part of it."

She stared at him. "For a person with your talent you have an unbelievable inferiority complex."

"You think so?"

"I'd never realized it before," she said seriously. "What the rest of us have been taking as sullenness is really shyness on your part."

"Figure it out any way you like," he said, bringing the car to a short stop before turning out onto the main highway.

"I will try to be more friendly from now on, I promise," she said.

"Because you're sorry for me?"

"Not really," she said. "Say it's because you have revealed yourself to me and I understand you better. And I think I like you better than I did."

"Three cheers!" he said in his mocking, bitter fashion. "In the meantime it's the triple-threat Barnabas you kiss goodnight."

Diana gasped. "Did everyone at Collinwood see us last night?"

"I can only answer for myself. And I kept discreetly in the shadows until the romantic scene had ended and you'd both vanished. Give me credit for that."

"I do," she said, her cheeks burning. "But I don't think much of your spying."

He laughed. "I wasn't exactly spying. Mary and I stayed at the chapel late, working out a new ending for the second act. I let her out at the door and then took the car around to the stables to park it. When I came back I saw you two."

"I'll accept your story if you just don't dwell on it."

"I won't," he promised. "But it seems to me you should know that at least two or three people in the village have assured me he's a vampire."

Diana shook her head. "That's utterly fantastic."

"Not according to them. They've always been wary of the Collins family. The list of suicides and killings at Collinwood make an impressive total. And all kinds of ghosts play a part in the legends that have grown up about that old house. I've gotten an idea for a new ballet by being here."

She smiled thinly. "I'm glad the silly talk has done some good."

"Fellow I met over a beer in the Blue Whale solemnly assured me that the reason Barnabas never appears in the daytime is because he sleeps in his coffin during the daylight hours. And he further claimed that Barnabas has to drink human blood to keep himself a vampire. That's the reason he goes around attacking all those young women."

Diana gave Stefan a disdainful look. "I'm sure you both had too many of those beers or you'd never have talked so wildly."

"I think this fellow believed what he was telling me," Stefan said.

63

"That doesn't mean any intelligent person has to believe it," she replied.

But the conversation did worry her. She refused to believe that the man she had fallen in love with was anything but what he seemed. To her he was a charming English gentleman and she couldn't picture him as being one of the walking dead. It was too monstrous!

They arrived at the hospital shortly after ten. Stefan went up to Eleanor's room with her. The dark-haired girl was sitting propped up against pillows and looked pale but better than Diana had expected. There were only a few minor scratches on one cheek and she ruefully complained of a small bump on her head which her long hair concealed. Stefan remained in the room long enough to wish the young dancer a speedy recovery and then rather embarrassedly left to wait for Diana in the lobby downstairs.

When the two girls were alone, Eleanor smiled at Diana and said, "You know he's rather sweet. And I've always thought he was cold and arrogant."

Diana nodded. "I'm just beginning to really understand him."

The dark girl said. "It was good of you to come."

She studied her with serious eyes. "Everyone has been worried about you," she said. "And I've felt especially guilty."

"Why?" Eleanor stared at her.

She made a tiny futile gesture. "I felt I might have in some way been to blame for what happened to you."

"Why should you think that?"

She looked directly at the injured girl. "I did introduce you to Barnabas Collins."

"So?"

"There are stories about him. About girls who've been attacked at night and a red mark left on their throats. They claimed you had a red mark on your throat."

Eleanor's pretty face registered annoyance. "I know," she said. "The police have been here and asked me a lot of silly questions about that. There's no mark on my throat now," she said, holding up her chin for Diana to see. "And if there was, it must have happened in the fall."

Diana felt relief. "I didn't put any stock in the gossip," she said. "But I wanted to ask you frankly what hap-

64

pened. Did you meet Barnabas again that night after we parted?"

Eleanor looked embarrassed. "Why do you ask?"

"Because he seemed to like you. To show a special interest in you."

The dark girl blushed. "We did meet about a half-hour later. He walked with me for a short distance. We had a pleasant talk. Then he went his way and I went mine."

Diana was ashamed that she should feel jealous of the other girl but she did. She tried to dismiss her feelings but wasn't too successful at it. In a taut voice, she asked, "Did he kiss you?"

A troubled look had come into the dark girl's lovely eyes. "I'm not sure."

Diana's eyebrows lifted. "Wouldn't you remember if he had?"

"Ordinarily, yes," Eleanor said. "But everything that happened that night is jumbled in my memory. It's because of the fall. I know we talked a long while and strolled arm in arm. He was very nice and he could have kissed me. I remember when we parted I was very happy, almost ecstatically happy, but I don't remember what he said or did. I thought I was walking back to the farmhouse but I went in the wrong direction. I heard the waves washing on the beach and I knew I must be on the cliffs."

"Why didn't you turn back?"

"I meant to," the dark-haired girl said with fear on her pretty face as she recalled that moment. "And then something or someone came up behind me and gave me a push and I fell over the cilff. That's the last I remember."

"You're sure you were pushed?"

"I don't know!" Eleanor said with terror in her eyes. "Perhaps there was a struggle. But I didn't see anyone. It was as though some invisible force had opposed itself to me and finally hurled me down on the rocks."

Diana frowned. "The truth is you haven't any clear memory of what went on."

"Yes. But I'm sure Barnabas had nothing to do with it. I'd left him a good while before my accident."

"I see," she said quietly. "By the way, he was very upset about your injury and asked that I mention him to you."

Eleanor smiled. "Please thank him for me."

Diana stood there rather awkwardly. Then she asked, "When will you be released?"

"The doctor says in a week. And tell Mary he said there's no reason why I can't take my place in the show again then."

"I will," she promised. "Though I don't think you should force yourself."

"I'm all right." Eleanor insisted. "And tell Barnabas I'll look forward to seeing him again and talking with him."

"Yes," Diana said. She only remained with the dark girl for a few minutes longer. Then she left her to rejoin Stefan in the lobby for the drive back to Collinwood.

She was surprised and upset by Eleanor's account of the night of her accident. It was all too clear the pretty dark girl had no good memory of what had exactly happened. At any rate, she had exonerated Barnabas of any blame in the matter. But could her account be depended on?

Diana didn't know. Eleanor was unaware of Diana's feelings for Barnabas and seemed ready to embark on a romance with him herself. Had Barnabas encouraged this? Was he really a kind of monster preying on innocents like Eleanor for the blood he needed to sustain his vampire's existence? Diana hated herself for thinking such thoughts and quickly suppressed them.

She was positive that Barnabas had done nothing wrong, that Eleanor had become infatuated with him in a perfectly understandable and normal way. Either the dark girl had had too much to drink at the party and stumbled over the cliff, or she'd been attacked by somebody else and shoved over. And if this latter should be true, who was to blame? The idea of the mysterious ghost at once came to mind. She firmly pushed it aside as she met Stefan in the lobby.

The long-haired composer looked comfortingly human as he said, "Well, what was all the long conversation up there about?"

She managed a smile. "Girl talk."

"I'll bet," he said dryly. "She didn't look too bad to me."

"No. She hopes to return to the company next week."

"She's one of the best dancers in the ensemble," he said.

"Mary will be glad to know she's coming back."

The drive to Collinwood didn't seem to take so long on the return trip. For one thing the weather had improved. The drizzle had ended and the fog was drifting out to sea, although it still hung over the ocean in thick white clouds at various spots. She and Stefan became more friendly as they discussed the ballet and other things of mutual interest. When he let her out before the front door of Collinwood the sun had broken through the clouds. She thanked him and went inside.

Rehearsals were resumed in the chapel that afternoon. With the return of the sun it became humid. Mary was in one of her most demanding moods and several times went up on the stage and danced sections of the solo parts herself to explain the way she wanted them interpreted. Watching the frail old woman dance was a remarkable experience. Diana forgot the age of the veteran ballet star as she marveled at the beauty of her interpretation. In the flowing chiffon robe of white that she invariably wore, the old woman had undeniable grace. It reminded Diana of several times when she'd witnessed dance solos by the famous Ruth St. Denis towards the end of her career.

Stefan labored at the piano as the rehearsal continued on through the long afternoon. There was a definite feud going on between the male stars of the company, Alex Carter and Peter Norrad. She knew that while it included their professional work it went far beyond that. The main cause of their hatred for each other was Mavis Norrad. She still spent much of her offstage time with Alex, while her husband would stand silent and glowering in the background.

It had reached the point now where neither of the two men spoke to each other. All the company were wise to what was going on, but Mary Wentworth seemed not to notice it. She was appreciative of Peter Norrad's talents and had often given him credit for training Mavis to reach stardom. But the old woman also was deeply grateful to Alex Carter for suggesting the company play at Collinwood for the summer and making all the arrangements for them.

During one short break in the rehearsal period Diana and Stefan met outside. The young composer's long hair was looped down on his forehead and perspiration shone on his sensitive face. He looked ugly.

In a taut voice, he said, "I could twist the neck of that Mavis. If she keeps on there'll be a major row between Alex and Peter and that'll be the end of my ballet."

She smiled at him thinly. "Don't forget Mavis is also one of the stars. If you killed her the show couldn't go on."

"Of course it could," he told her. "You're understudying the part. I've watched you and I'll bet with a few performances you'd be better than she is."

Diana gave him a look of mock reproach. "Just the same, don't finish her off on my account. I'm happy doing a minor role."

They were standing a little distance from the chapel and the young composer glared back to where Mavis and Alex were talking together in a conspiratorial manner near the entrance to the stone building.

"She should be stopped some way before she wrecks everything," he murmured angrily.

Then the young man acting as stage manager came out and called them inside to rehearsal again. Diana did her final scene in the second act and at once left the darkened auditorium for some fresh air and sunshine. The ballet would give its first public performance in a little more than a week. Then they would soon know whether it was going to be the success they'd hoped. Mary Wentworth had arranged with some of the critics to come down from Boston and New York to review the show.

Diana stood by the door of the vine-covered stone chapel for a moment relaxing. There would be rehearsal again that night. She hoped it wouldn't be too long and she wouldn't be kept late. She needed to have a long chat with Barnabas and he never appeared until dusk. This thought brought back all the horrifying accusations that had been voiced against him. While she refused to believe any of them they remained a source of concern for her.

Inside they had come to another scene in the ballet calling for the haunting waltz theme. Stefan played the lilting melody on the piano in a loving fashion. She knew how much the ballet meant to its intense young composer and guessed that his rage at Mavis for endangering the project with her flirtation had been genuine enough. Stefan literally would be willing to remove any hindrance to the ballet being performed. Even if that hindrance should turn out to be his own half-sister.

There was no love lost between the two. Diana left the entrance of the chapel to walk around to the back and the old cemetery. She was anxious to see if some one at Collinwood had arranged for the despoiled grave of Mario Renzie to be filled in again. As she neared the small cemetery a strange feeling came over her, a feeling that danger was close at hand.

Forcing herself to continue on, she went to the grave of the young sailor who was reputed to have become the avenging specter known as the mysterious ghost. The earth had been neatly put back into the grave, and there was a grim air of quiet about its surroundings. Fighting back the increasing panic within her she moved on between the neat rows of grassy mounds and weathered gravestones.

She did not really know why she had come to the lonely old cemetery or why she was remaining there. It was as if a phantom hand had seized her by the arm and guided her to this place of death. She continued on to the far side of the graveyard before she came to a halt.

What brought her to a halt and caused her eyes to widen with horror was the sight of another defiled grave. This one bore a headstone stating that the remains of Abel Collins rested there. A chill went through her as she recalled that Abel Collins had been father to Anya and later a supposed victim of the avenging Mario's ghost. Had the ghost been at work again?

She would have screamed out her fear had the sight of the opened grave not frozen her with revulsion and terror. For deep down in the ground in a corner of the grave, a bleached white skull lay starkly against the black earth grinning up at her!

CHAPTER SIX

She felt she would faint. The blazing sun and the ugly sight of the weathered gravestone, the pile of loose earth and the dark grave with the macabre skull gazing up at her combined to overwhelm her. She swayed slightly by the open grave, not able to help herself.

And then the voice came to her, nasal, middle-aged and male. "Kind of a shocking sight, miss," the voice said in dry sympathy.

Her horrified eyes lifted from the opening of the grave to focus on a short, rather stout man in a drab gray suit, white shirt and narrow black tie. He wore a faded hat that was battered with age, and under it there was a lined, tanned face. The face was not unfriendly and not even of features. The man had bushy gray eyebrows and a Roman nose. His eyes were sharp and wrinkles showed at their corners. Those sharp eyes were fixed on her now.

In a tight voice she managed to ask, "Who are you?"

"Haig's the name," he said mildly. "Chief Joshua Haig from Ellsworth. Since I'm responsible for the law in this county I thought I'd come over here and take a look at the cemetery myself."

She stared at him a long minute and then looked numbly at the grave. "This is a new one. It wasn't dug up before."

Chief Haig came over and peered into the grave. He raised his eyes to her. "They went all the way down, didn't they? That appears to be Abel's bones down there."

"It's horrible!" she gasped.

"Yep. It's nasty all right," the chief of the Ellsworth police agreed in his calm fashion. "I guess you're the gal who found the other grave open."

"I did."

He was regarding her with more than ordinary interest. "That's real strange," he observed. "Real strange! You spend a lot of your time in graveyards?"

The question startled her. She shook her head. "No!"

He nodded, keeping his eyes on her. "Reason I asked is because you're the one first around to notice these open graves."

"We're rehearsing in the chapel," she said. "I sometimes come here in my free moments. It's so near."

"Yep, it is," he agreed, showing no expression. "But I guess you are the only one who takes any interest in this place. None of the others barge in here to tumble onto open graves."

It was a simple statement of fact, and she saw that she had to offer some explanation or be eyed with suspicion. She said, "One of the Collins family told me about the cemetery. And about the legend of Mario and Anya. And the fact they were buried here."

"I see," the chief said. "This Abel was Anya's father, but I expect you'd know that too."

"Yes."

"So you sort of got hooked by that ghost story," the chief said with what was for him a show of interest. "You'd sure think some ghost was after these graves. One who knew how to handle a shovel."

"What does it mean?"

"Somebody's crazy," the short, stout man said. "We get all kinds of types here in summer."

"You're blaming it on some outsider?"

"Yes and no," the chief said cannily. "What I'm saying is that whoever did it wasn't too right in the head. It could be anybody, even one of the Collins family or somebody in your ballet outfit."

"I think you're right. It has to be a stranger. Probably that Hank, whom Roger Collins let go before we arrived."

The chief rubbed his chin speculatively and gave a regretful glance down into the grave again. "Only trouble with that theory is that fellas like that Hank usually ain't crazy. A fella like that don't look for a lot of shovel work. It took some hard labor to dig up this grave."

"Then who do you suspect?"

He frowned. "That's a good question and I don't rightly have as good an answer," he was ready to admit. "Now, you said one of the Collins family first told you about this

71

place and got you interested in it."

"Yes," she said faintly.

"Which Collins was it?"

She had a wild impulse to lie and claim it was Elizabeth who'd told her about the cemetery and the legend. Take a chance that he would accept her word and not question the older woman. But after a few seconds consideration she knew this could wedge her in a corner where there would have to be additional lies to explain her own actions. This would eventually become a trap for her. Better to tell the truth.

"Barnabas Collins told me about the legend and the cemetery," she finally said.

"Barnabas?" he repeated owl-like after her. Then he brightened a little. "Oh, I guess you mean that cousin of theirs who is over here from England."

"Yes."

The short man took a step back from the grave and moved around to stand beside her. "So Barnabas was the one told you all about the graves and ghosts."

"He did," she admitted faintly.

"Well, Barnabas should know," he said in his easy fashion. "Though I'd be more inclined to call him a stranger rather than family."

"But he is one of the family," she defended Barnabas.

"Yes and no," was the chief's opinion. "And he's an odd one, that's for sure. People in the village give him plenty of space if he comes in of an evening. I guess maybe you've heard some of the things they're saying about him."

"I call all that talk ridiculous," she retorted angrily. Her rage coming up had dispelled a good deal of her feeling of faintness.

"Well, I don't exactly go for that kind of gossip," the chief admitted. "But he does do some strange things. Like when I went to call on him on my way over here he was too busy to see me. Told his servant I could come back later." He rummaged in his jacket pocket and finally produced a wrinkled slip of white paper. "There it is," he said triumphantly as he passed it to her.

Diana read the message. It said, "To whom it may concern, I am engaged in demanding work and cannot leave it for anyone. Please leave your card or message with my man, Hare."

"I've always had warm receptions from both the locals and the summer people," he said. "I've never been given such a cold shoulder as this before. Makes me kind of prejudiced about this Barnabas."

"Why should it?" she asked nervously. "He's doing research into local history and doesn't want to be interrupted."

"I'm doing some research myself," the police chief said with a wise look on his plain face. "And I figure it's pretty important. I could have made a fuss and insisted I see Mr. Barnabas Collins if I'd wanted to. But I'm not anxious to cause the Collins family trouble just yet."

Diana had gotten over the worst of her fainting feeling. Now she moved further away from the open grave. "I hope you find whoever is doing this and stop them," she said, changing the subject.

The chief nodded. "I'll find out," he promised. "May take a little time, though." He pulled out a battered black notebook from an inside pocket. Consulting it, he asked, "You're Miss Diana Samson, aren't you?"

"Yes."

Chief Haig made a notation in the book with a stubby lead pencil. Then he closed the book and put it away. "I might be wanting to talk to you later," he told her. "I've got some other angles to investigate."

"I'm living at Collinwood."

"So, I'll know where to find you," he said. "And if I were you I'd be careful around here after dark."

"Thank you," she said.

"And I wouldn't linger in this cemetery," he advised. "Never know what kind of lunatic might be over there in the bushes watching you and what crazy idea they could get in their head."

And he made it a point to escort her back to the entrance of the chapel. The rehearsal was still going on though she knew it must be near an end. The chief stuck his head in the door for a minute and watched one of the group scenes. Then he glanced at her with a smile of disbelief.

"This is a new kind of a show for Collinsport," he said.

73

"Don't you think they'll like it?" she asked.

He shrugged. "Hard to say from what I saw just now. When I get a free night I'll bring the missus down and see the whole performance."

"You must do that," she encouraged him.

He tipped his faded hat and trudged off, leaving her in a worried state. She had the feeling the wily representative of the law was suspicious of her, as well as distrustful of Barnabas and his motives. She was positive she would hear from him again and it might not be a pleasant experience. She worried more about Barnabas than she did for herself.

The rehearsal ended and she went back to Collinwood. The evening call wasn't until eight at the chapel. She felt the need of some air and sunshine and so went for a stroll along the cliffs. When she came back she walked through the garden and accidentally overheard an argument between Alex and Mavis. They were separated from her only by a hedge which rose above head level. Mavis apparently heard Diana's footsteps on the gravel path and at once hurried off without looking back to see who it was. A moment later Diana found herself confronted by Alex, smiling superciliously.

"So it was you we heard," he said.

"I didn't mean to interrupt," she told him.

His smile was bleak. "We were having an argument. I suppose you listened and know what it was about."

She frowned indignantly. "I certainly didn't listen."

"It doesn't matter," he said. "Mavis is a little fool. She thinks we should run off together. She doesn't stop to think what opening in this ballet could mean for both our careers."

Diana said, "Beyond that, isn't there Peter to consider? He is her husband."

Alex looked self-satisfied. "She doesn't love him. She plans to leave him no matter what."

"I'd rather not hear any of your sordid stories," she protested and attempted to move on, but he neatly blocked her way, his face shadowed.

"You don't think I'm good enough for you, do you?"

"I try not to think about you at all," she said angrily. "Please stop being ridiculous!" She again attempted to move around him.

He reached out and gripped her arm. "Be nice to me," he ordered her, "or you may wind up sorry."

"Let me go!" she cried and, wrenching herself free of him, ran towards the house.

She at once went up to Mary Wentworth's room and found her seated in an armchair, staring blankly out a window at the ocean. Huddled and dejected, the elderly ballet director looked her age for a change. Diana had some hesitation about disturbing her with an account of the misbehavior of the brash Alex Carter, but she felt she should. Seating herself near the old woman, she launched a detailed account of the way he was acting.

The white-haired Mary Wentworth listened in silence. When Diana had ended, she said, "I knew something of what he is up to, but for the good of the company I've tried to be lenient with him."

"It may not work," she worried.

The old woman's sharp black eyes fixed on her. "Are you jealous of Mavis? Do you love Alex?"

"I do not," she exclaimed in surprise. "I have never liked him. He's far too cheap a person."

"He cannot help his background," the old lady said patiently. "He had had little formal education and not too long ago he was a side-show barker with a carnival. He has come a long way and needed great ambition to do it."

"Yet he's never basically changed from that sort of person," Diana argued. "And he's apt to return to that kind of life and drag Mavis with him."

"He'll do nothing to hurt the company," was the veteran star's prediction. Then giving her a knowing look, she asked, "What about you and your romance with this strange character, Barnabas?"

Diana resented the question. "My friendship with Barnabas is a private thing," she insisted.

"Mrs. Stoddard is worried about it," Mary Wentworth said gravely. "You must have heard what the people here say about Barnabas Collins."

"I don't listen to such talk!"

"Perhaps you should," Mary said meaningfully. "When we came here I told you I could sense the presence of the supernatural in this house. I sense it more than ever before now. And it spells danger."

Diana left the old woman feeling she had made no progress at all. And she was further upset by the criticism of Barnabas on all sides. It was too unfair. The evening rehearsal session was suddenly canceled because Stefan had not been able to complete a new musical passage he was substituting in the second act. With the evening free Diana at once longed to talk to Barnabas.

She left the main house of Collinwood and walked back to the old house where Barnabas was staying. By the time she reached the smaller, brick structure it was on the edge of dusk. She felt that surely Barnabas would have his work finished and be ready to see her, and she hoped he wouldn't resent her coming to his door without an invitation.

Mounting the several stone steps, she knocked on the oak door. It was at least several minutes before the door was opened a crack and the ugly face of Hare peered out at her from the shadows of the hall.

Assuming a smile, she spoke slowly. "It's Miss Samson. Miss Diana Samson and I'd like to speak with Mr. Collins."

The ugly, beard-stubbled face held an impassive expression as the mute servant listened to her. Then the door was closed abruptly and she stood there in a sorry state of mind waiting to see what would now happen.

At last footsteps approached and the door was opened again, this time fully to reveal Barnabas standing there in his caped coat.

"Diana!" he said, surprised. "What brings you here?"

"The rehearsal was canceled and I was anxious to see you," she said.

He at once showed concern. "Has anything serious happened?"

"No," she said. "But there have been some puzzling developments. And Chief Haig from Ellsworth was here."

Barnabas nodded grimly. "I know that. He left a written message for me with Hare."

She felt awkward standing on the steps. "May I come in for a moment?"

He gave her a rather furtive look before stepping back and saying, "Of course."

He escorted her to an open door. It led to a well fur-

76

nished living room filled with antique furniture. Candles flickered in silver candlesticks on two of the several tables giving the room a soft intimate atmosphere. Barnabas indicated a divan and she sat on it.

Seating himself beside her, he asked, "Now tell me what has been going on."

She did, concentrating on what Eleanor had told her, and of her discovery of Abel's grave being dug up as the newest example of vandalism in the small cemetery behind the chapel.

Barnabas frowned. "It has to be the work of some stranger."

"Then you rule out evil spirits?"

He looked at her. "The chief is right. You should stay away from that graveyard."

"But it fascinates me," she protested. "I somehow knew another grave would be defiled and that it would be that of Abel Collins."

The flickering candlelight gave his melancholy features a brooding expression. "You must forget about the legend," he warned her.

"You can't forget such things at Collinwood," she said. Glancing around, she added, "Take this room, for instance. It is like one you'd be in a century or two ago. No electricity and only the fireplace for heat! And the furniture is ancient."

Barnabas smiled sadly. "Elizabeth and Roger have never taken much interest in this old place. It's fortunate it is in as good a state as you find it. When I first returned here a few years ago I had it restored but I couldn't install lights or heat without their permission. Since I remain here only a short time on any of my visits, I didn't need such modern conveniences."

She was staring at him. "Eleanor claimed you and she met the night of her accident but that you had nothing to do with what happened. I have an idea she may have fallen in love with you."

"I think you are wrong in that," Barnabas said quietly.

"She is certainly fond of you."

"And I like her," the man on the divan beside her said. "Eleanor is an interesting girl."

Summoning her courage she looked at him directly.

"Barnabas, you have never told me anything about yourself. I mean about your past. Surely you have been in love, no doubt many times. Have you ever been engaged or married?"

His handsome face showed a thoughtful expression. "If I'm to be honest I must admit I have been in love," he said quietly. "And I once was engaged to a girl here, but I have never married."

"Who was the girl?" Diana wanted to know. "Does she still live here?"

Barnabas said, "She is dead. I'd rather not discuss it."

"I'm sorry," she said.

"Why do you suddenly ask me all these questions?" he said, his deep-set eyes fixed on her.

She smiled forlornly. "Because I'm in love with you and would like to marry you. And I know so little about you."

He took her hands in his, and again she was conscious of their coldness. His eyes met hers solemnly. "We should be friends and nothing more," he said. "There can be no future for us."

Alarm crossed her pretty face. "Why do you tell me that? And why does everyone else warn me against you? The things they whisper about you can't be true! You're not a vampire! I won't believe it!"

Barnabas smiled faintly. "If you won't believe it then that settles it."

Diana stood up. "Let's go someplace where there are people and maybe music and we can forget about all our problems."

Barnabas got to his feet. "I'm afraid the choice in town is rather limited. But there is the Blue Whale Tavern."

"I've heard Maggie and Carolyn mention it," Diana said. "I'd like to go there."

"It's quite a distance to the village," Barnabas reminded her.

"We can find a car," she said. And she gave him a questioning frown. "How do you usually get there?"

"Various ways when I'm alone," he said evasively.

"Stefan has a car," she said. "He's busy working on the ballet score tonight, but I'm sure he'll allow us to use it. I'll ask him for the keys."

The young composer gave them to her with a warning not to drive too fast. Within a quarter-hour she and Barnabas were on their way to the Blue Whale. The village was full of tourists and they had to drive all the way down to the wharf to find a parking place. Then they walked up the steep hill of the main street towards the brilliant blue and red neon lights of the tavern.

As they walked with arms linked, she said, "You must have seen a lot of changes in Collinsport."

"Sometimes I barely recognize it," he agreed.

"When were you first here?" she asked.

He glanced at her. "What was that?"

"I asked when you first came here from England. I believe you've made many visits to Collinwood."

Instead of replying he nodded towards the entrance of the Blue Whale and said, "Isn't that one of the young men from your company?"

She stared ahead and saw Alex escorting Mavis into the tavern. At once all her old apprehensions concerning the two and the effect their flirtation could have on the company returned.

She said, "Yes. And he's with Mavis again."

"The wife of your other male star," Barnabas said. "Isn't that a troublesome situation?"

"It's bad," she admitted.

Barnabas opened the door of the tavern for her and they went inside. The long, dimly lighted saloon was thick with tobacco smoke and every table seemed to be occupied. A huge, garish, neon-tubed juke box at the very rear of the drinking place blared out a noisy rock and roll number. Even the bar was fairly well crowded.

At their entrance it seemed every eye in the place was turned to them. She knew that Barnabas attracted this kind of attention wherever he went in Collinsport and felt a trifle embarrassed.

He appeared not to notice the curious stares and took her over to an empty place at the bar. "We'll have to be satisfied to stand for a little," he said. "You were anxious to see a lot of people. Now you have."

"Too many!" she protested, glancing around to try and see where Mavis and Alex had gone. After a moment she spotted them in the second seat from the rear. They appeared to be in earnest conversation and hadn't seen her.

Barnabas ordered for them. The bartender seemed to know him and served them in an overly polite fashion. It struck her that Barnabas in his caped coat and with his regal bearing had produced a feeling of awe among the local people.

They'd only been standing there a few minutes when Peter Norrad came striding through the tavern door with an agitated expression on his haggard face. He at once saw her and came over to her.

"Is Mavis in here?" he demanded.

She gave him a pleading look. "I wouldn't worry about her," she said.

"I asked you a question," he said coldly.

"It would be better if you ignored her and Alex," she said. "I'm sure there is nothing serious between them."

Peter glared at her impatiently. Then he gave his attention to the rest of the long room and almost at once saw Mavis and Alex. He marched down the length of the tavern and halted at their booth. Diana had no idea of what was being said but she could tell that Peter was addressing the two angrily.

Abruptly Peter left the table and strode back towards the door of the tavern. This time he didn't even pause to speak to her but went past without looking her way. He went out and slammed the door after him.

Barnabas gave her a knowing look. "He's not too happy," he said.

"I know," she agreed worriedly. "I hope he doesn't do anything rash."

Barnabas said, "Perhaps I should go out and try to reason with him."

"You hardly know him," she said. "It might only make things worse. He's very proud."

Barnabas said, "I can be tactful. Let me try." And without giving her a chance to stop him, he left her and followed Peter out of the tavern.

She stood there considering it all. And then she stared into the mirror that ran the length of the bar and saw her pale, troubled face reflected in it along with the reflections of the others who were standing there. And she suddenly realized that she had been party to a strange experience and hadn't been aware of it until this moment.

All the time Barnabas had been standing at her side there had been no hint of him in the mirror. It was as if she'd been there alone. It was hard to believe but she knew it was true. His reflection simply had not registered in the mirror!

She forgot all her other worries in the shock of this discovery. What could it mean? Had it been a kind of illusion, or was it a grim warning? She faintly recalled having read a ghost story somewhere in which an apparently normal person had been revealed as a ghost when his image did not show in a mirror. All her fears and doubts about Barnabas returned and she felt faint.

"Evening, Miss Samson. Didn't look to see you here," a voice at her elbow said. She turned to see Chief of Police Joshua Haig studying her with his shrewd eyes.

She swallowed hard. "I'm just leaving," she said.

The chief's eyebrows raised. "Aren't you going to wait for your friend to return? I saw him go out."

Diana wondered if the police chief had also noticed that there had been no reflection of Barnabas in the bar mirror. She hoped not. She wanted to get outside and question Barnabas at once.

She said, "We're ready to leave."

"Tell him I'm still waiting to have that little chat with him," the chief said, but he made no motion to follow her as she left the bar.

Outside she stood on the sidewalk trying to see which way Barnabas might have gone, but though there were quite a few people in the street, there was no sign of him. Nor any sign of Peter Norrad.

She didn't want to wait there too long as she feared that Chief Haig might follow her out and complicate matters. The quick succession of the unexpected had left her in a harried state. She finally decided she would walk back down to the wharf where she'd left the car. Perhaps Barnabas had seen the chief and, wanting to avoid him, had decided to wait for her there.

Fairly running down the steep main street, she reached the dark area where her car was parked and searched for some sign of the man she had come to love standing in the shadows. But he wasn't there. The area was deserted. She began to feel uneasily alone in the darkness and quickly unlocked the car and got in.

She backed out of the parking space and headed the small sedan up the steep hill of the main street. As she drove she looked for some glimpse of Barnabas and Peter Norrad, but she had no luck. She continued driving until she'd passed the main business district, including the hotel, and had left the busy, well-lighted section of the street.

Suddenly two figures loomed on the right. Barnabas with a girl she'd never seen before at his side. She quickly braked the car and turned to see what their reaction had been. But in the space of a few seconds they had vanished. The road was empty of anyone!

CHAPTER SEVEN

It was Carolyn who returned from the village the following evening with word that one of the local girls had been
attacked the night before and had later been found wandering near the wharves. Diana was standing with
Elizabeth in the garden when the girl came to them full
of excitement.

"Everyone in the village is upset about it," Carolyn
said.

Elizabeth looked worried. "And the girl wasn't able to
identify who attacked her?"

"No," Carolyn said. "She was just as confused as the
others were. And she had the same red mark on her
throat. You can guess what some of them are saying."

Her mother frowned. "I suppose they are bringing up
the vampire legend and accusing Barnabas of being the
criminal."

"Something like that," Carolyn said unhappily. "I told
anyone who mentioned it to me that Cousin Barnabas is a
fine man."

Diana asked, "When is this supposed to have happened?"

"No one seems quite sure," Carolyn told her. "But it
had to be after ten o'clock. The girl was with a friend until
then. After that she started home alone."

Diana knew it had to be around that time, for it was
about then that Barnabas had become restless, and using
the excuse of following Peter Norrad, had gone off on his
own. Later she'd seen him at the edge of the road with a
girl who was a stranger to her. She could no longer close
her eyes to the fact that Barnabas was the one preying on
the village girls. And this was reinforced by the knowledge
that his reflection had not shown in the bar mirror. It
seemed he was no normal human. He had complained of
an illness. She now thought she knew what it must be.

Barnabas was one of the living dead. The tall handsome Britisher bore the vampire taint.

Strangely she found it made no difference in her love for him. Indeed her thoughts were all concerned with how she could help him break the curse that was shadowing his life and bring him back to normalcy. Surely there must be a way, and Diana determined that she would find it.

Elizabeth and Carolyn went on into the house together, leaving her alone in the garden. She had an idea the two wanted to leave her behind to they could talk more frankly about the plight of Barnabas. They little suspected that she knew more than they did and that she was deeply in love with the striking dark-haired man.

She sat down on one of the several green wooden benches in the garden and thought about it all. She'd read that vampires needed fresh supplies of human blood to survive. And it must be that thirst which sent Barnabas stalking young women on dark nights. That dreadful thirst which made him a phantom caught between life and death. These thoughts were tormenting her when she heard footsteps approaching on the gravel path and she looked up to see Alex standing before her with a sneer.

"I saw you with your friend Barnabas in the tavern last night," he said. "What do you think of him now?"

"It's not any of your business," she told him angrily.

"All the village have him branded as a vampire. Did he leave you last night for that girl?"

Diana jumped up. "I don't want to hear any more about it."

He laughed nastily. "But you're bound to. So better prepare yourself."

She hurried away from him. Rehearsal was to begin late at around nine o'clock. And she hoped to talk to Barnabas before then so she walked directly to the old house. It was dusk when she reached there and Barnabas was standing on the steps of the house.

When she came up to him, she said, "I hoped I'd find you here."

He frowned. "Shouldn't you be rehearsing?"

"Not until later," she said. Her eyes met his. "I saw you last night. I know what happened and what you are. And I

84

still love you and want to help you."

It was a startling declaration that made Barnabas stand there for a moment in silence. Then he said, "You sound very sure of yourself."

"I am," she told him. "If you bear the vampire curse, it is not your fault. Somehow we'll fight it together."

Barnabas smiled sadly. "Your belief in me is touching," he said. "But have you really faced up to the sacrifice it can mean on your part?"

"I think so," she said.

He gave her an odd look, then said, "Come inside for a moment."

This time he conducted her downstairs to the cellar rather than to the living room. He carried a candle for light. She went down the worn stone steps and followed him along the earthen floor of the cellar. At the very end they came to a door opening to a room bare except for a coffin on a stand. Barnabas moved close to the coffin, holding the candle high enough so she could take in her surroundings.

"This is where I've been condemned to spend my days," he said, standing by the coffin. "After what you've told me you have a right to see it."

Fearfully she stared at the empty coffin with its satin lining and felt the icy chill of the room. This was truly an abode of the dead.

Turning to him, she asked, "When you rest in this do you have dreams? Or is it a kind of coma that comes over you?"

"It is more a coma," he said sadly but proudly. "The chances of my finding a cure are extremely slim. I can't ask you to gamble on them."

"But I want to!"

Looking at him, she saw his shadow on the wall, enlarged in the flickering flame of the candle.

"When did you first guess about me?"

"I was first sure last night when your reflection did not show in the bar mirror," she said.

Barnabas nodded. "I'd hoped you wouldn't notice."

"Then you left so quickly. Later I saw you with that girl." She paused. "I suppose when you met Eleanor that night you took blood from her in the same way."

"But I wasn't responsible for her fall," he said. "That happened afterwards."

"She would still be in a dazed state."

"I suppose so," Barnabas admitted. "But somebody else must have met her and tried to kill her."

"She says the same thing. But who?"

His eyes met hers. "The same person who has attacked you."

"Or the same phantom," she corrected him.

"Possibly."

"We needn't worry about Eleanor," she said. "She's recovering. What are we going to do for you? The village people are upset and ready to turn on you. Dare you risk remaining here?"

"I don't want to leave until I am sure you are safe."

"We could leave together after the ballet season ends," she suggested. "But the way things are going you could be in serious trouble by then."

His deep-set eyes searched hers. "Would you really sacrifice your life to devote yourself to me?"

"Yes."

Barnabas took her in his arms and touched his cold lips gently to hers. With infinite compassion he smiled at her, then he indicated the empty coffin beside them with a nod. "You almost make me forget the lonely hours I've spent in there, and the ones I must spend in it over the years ahead."

"There must be a way to save you from that," she said, looking up at him.

"We'll worry about that later," he said. "I need to have a private talk with Elizabeth now, and you will be late for your rehearsal. You'd better go on ahead and I'll join you at the chapel."

"You promise?" she asked, reluctant to let him go.

"I promise," he assured her, and they left the room together.

Darkness was cloaking the countryside as they emerged from the old house. Diana leaned close to him and gave a tiny shiver. Remembrance of that room in the cellar together with all the other horrors she'd experienced at Collinwood made her uneasy.

Barnabas gave her a worried look. "I shouldn't send you on alone."

"It will be all right," she promised. "The others will all be there by now. And the walk is by the main house and not too lonely."

"I'll go with you part of the way," he decided. "At least until we are within sight of the chapel."

"There's no need," she protested, but he remained with her.

He only left her when the lights from the chapel and the farmhouse beyond showed through the darkness. He turned to go back to Collinwood while she continued on to the chapel. There were neither stars nor moon showing, and the night seemed unusually still.

As she neared the entrance to the chapel she thought she heard a sound from the nearby bushes, the same bushes where she had seen that ugly, scowling face the day of the attack on her. She glanced towards the bushes in sudden fear, but there was no sign of movement in the shadows. Because of the fright, she hurried on.

As soon as she reached the entrance to the chapel she knew that something was wrong. There was no sound of the piano from inside and no murmur of voices. It struck her that the rehearsal might have been canceled at the last moment after she'd left Collinwood. Gingerly she stepped inside the dark building, hardly knowing what to expect. Then above her in the bell tower, the bell suddenly began to toll. She glanced up automatically with a shiver of fear. As she stared up into the grim black heights of the chapel's vaulted roof someone brushed against her in the dark and shoved her so violently she stumbled forward!

She gave an alarmed cry at the same time she heard scurrying footsteps on the stone steps and then moving off into the night. She recovered herself and stood trembling in the center aisle. It was only then her eyes sought the stage and the faint light from some concealed overhead spot that illuminated it. And in the feeble blue light she saw something that made her gasp again.

A girl's body hung from part of the staging scaffold. The slim female figure's feet dangled a foot or so above the stage, while what looked like a white scarf was looped about her neck and the other end tied around a wooden overhead support. A chair rested on its side on the stage near the girl's feet, suggesting that she'd used it to hang herself, having kicked it aside in her death contortions.

Diana stood there frozen with shock and terror. It took her only a moment longer to recognize Mavis Norrad hanging there. She was paralyzed with her discovery. Where were the others? What had brought Mavis here alone? Had she committed suicide, or was it murder made to appear a self-inflicted death?

Her eyes had become more adjusted to the shadows of the ancient chapel and she was also aware that the bell in the chapel tower had become silent again. Yet she was positive it had tolled when she'd come in and had continued for at least a couple of minutes. All that had happened passed through her mind in a kind of slow-motion photography.

And then, just ahead of her on the slate floor of the chapel, she saw what looked like a crumpled heap of old clothes. She inched forward to it. Staring down, she saw that it was the motionless figure of Mary Wentworth, who appeared to be either unconscious or dead!

This second shocking discovery broke the spell of the first one. She wheeled around and ran from the chapel. Outside, she at once headed for the farmhouse. It seemed a world away, though the distance was really very short, and when she arrived there sobbing and gasping, she was met at the door by a puzzled Peter Norrad.

Peter took her in his arms. "What's wrong? Where have you been?"

"In the chapel, two bodies," she said, not knowing how to tell him about Mavis.

Others of the company had come crowding around them now, curious as to the reason for her hysteria. Peter held her by the arms and tried to get some further information from her.

"What's happened at the chapel?" he asked.

"Go and find out for yourself," she said.

Hurriedly turning her over to Stefan, he led a group of the others to the chapel. Stefan stared at her.

"We decided to rehearse here tonight," he said. "We were just going to work on one scene and didn't want to bother changing the setting at the chapel. We left word at the house for you. Mary walked back to the chapel to get her script. I offered to go for it, but she said she knew exactly where it was, so I didn't. We've been waiting for her to return."

Diana leaned weakly against him and closed her eyes. "She's back there on the floor. Mavis hanged herself. I think Mary went in and found her and fainted."

"Mavis hanged herself?" The young composer repeated this incredulously.

She opened her eyes and saw his pale, frightened face. "Either that or someone murdered her. She's hanging from one of the scenery supports."

"Mavis wouldn't kill herself!" he protested, as if by merely saying that she wouldn't the whole incident would be erased.

At that moment Peter returned, carrying Mary Wentworth in his arms. As he reached the door of the farmhouse he told Stefan, "Call the village for a doctor and the police."

Stefan eyed Mary's unconscious, limp figure in dismay. "Is she alive?"

"I think so," Peter said. "My wife is dead." He went on by them to place the old woman on a bed in one of the farmhouse bedrooms on the lower floor.

The others in the company learned the frightening news and a general state of confusion ensued. Diana sat with her head in her hands. She was still sitting there when Barnabas arrived.

He came to her. In a low voice, he said, "This is a bad business but I'm not surprised."

She looked up at him. "Do you think it was murder?"

"Chances are that it was," Barnabas said grimly. "Exactly what happened after I left you?"

She told him quickly and added, "The doctor is in with Mary now."

Barnabas asked, "Are you certain you heard the bell toll? I wasn't all that far away and I can't say that I noticed it."

"You must have without giving it attention," she insisted. "And whoever came down from the bell tower was the one who brushed by me and almost knocked me down!"

89

"Likely the murderer, who didn't want to be recognized," Barnabas said.

She was trembling now that it was over. "Perhaps," she agreed.

Stefan came to stand with them. The composer was pale and obviously shaken. "Have the police arrived at the chapel?"

"Not yet," Barnabas said.

Stefan eyed them grimly. "I got them on the phone. They're on their way. I suppose this is the end of the ballet. Mavis dead and Mary Wentworth seems to be near death."

"There was someone in the chapel when I got there," Diana told Stefan. "Whoever it was must have killed Mavis."

"It could have been suicide," Stefan said stubbornly. "There was an overturned chair by her feet."

Barnabas gave him a measured look. "Could that not have been deliberately placed there to throw us off? Make it look like suicide."

Stefan was angry. "If that's the case, we're finished," he said. "One of us has to be the murderer."

"Peter?" Barnabas questioned him. "After all, he was the wronged husband."

"Peter has collapsed in one of the bedrooms," Stefan said. "I don't think he'd be taking it that badly if he was responsible. There's no reason why he should feel it so. Mavis was cruel enough to him. But he loved her and I'll say he didn't murder her."

The sound of an approaching police siren ended the exchange. Stefan went off at once to meet the police at the chapel. Some of the young men and women of the company were already over there and a few stood around in the big farm kitchen, looking stunned.

Barnabas asked Diana, "Where's Alex Carter?"

"I guess he's one of those who stayed at the chapel," she said with a resigned look.

"He brought this all on," Barnabas said.

"I know," she sighed. "I'm afraid for Peter."

"Don't jump to conclusions," he warned her. "Are you positive you didn't get a look at whoever rushed by you and out of the chapel?"

90

She shook her head. "No. It was so unexpected."

An elderly man with a doctor's bag came out into the kitchen. He stared at them all and announced, "The old woman has come around. She's going to be all right. She's asking for Diana. Which one of you is Diana?"

She stood up at once. "I am," she said.

"You'd better go to her," the doctor advised. "Don't let her upset herself too much. I've given her a sedative, and once that begins to work, she'll fall asleep. I assume she can remain here for the night."

"There's no worry about that," Diana promised. "Whoever has the room will gladly let her have it."

"Good," the doctor said with a stern glance at Barnabas, as if he didn't much like seeing him there. "I'll come back to see her in the morning. I'm going on to the chapel now. I also happen to be the coroner in this county."

As he left, Diana said, "I'd better go to Miss Wentworth."

"May I go along?" Barnabas asked. As she hesitated, he added, "I'll be very quiet. I just want to stay in the background and hear what she has to say."

"I don't suppose it can do any harm," she said with a sigh.

She led the way to the small bedroom, located just off the kitchen and used by some of the girls of the ensemble. Mary's pale face merged with the white pillow uncannily.

She stepped quietly to the bedside and said, "It's Diana."

The old woman's eyelids fluttered and she looked up at her rather blankly. Then a gleam of fear came into the black eyes. "I saw you standing with Barnabas just before I went into the chapel," she said.

"I didn't notice you," Diana said, conscious that Barnabas was standing in the background and wondering what the old woman might be about to say.

"I was going to wait for you and then I decided against it," Mary continued weakly. "I went into the chapel alone and I saw Mavis. She was being lifted into the air by invisible hands."

Diana frowned at the startling words. "Lifted into the air?"

"Yes," Mary said. "I saw it. Some invisible force had taken hold of her. And in the next moment she was hanging there."

"It must have been a dreadful shock for you," Diana said in a comforting tone. She believed the old woman's story to be the result of shock and her drugged state.

"You know the legend of the girl Anya who hanged herself there?" the old woman said. "The ghost caused the same thing to happen to Mavis." She closed her eyes and turned her head away.

Diana stood in the softly lit room until she heard the regular breathing which indicated Mary had slipped off into a drugged sleep. She turned to Barnabas and touched a finger to her lips for silence. Then they both quietly went out of the room and closed the door after them.

Diana gazed at Barnabas with a puzzled air. "Of course, what she said just now was ridiculous."

Barnabas raised his eyebrows. "I wondered if you'd think that."

"She obviously went into the chapel and found Mavis hanging there and imagined the rest."

"Just as you imagined that knife dangling over your head on the same stage the night we first met," Barnabas said.

She hesitated, confused by the too vivid memory of that incident. Then she said, "I believe I really saw that knife."

"Then why dispute Miss Wentworth's story? Couldn't the same invisible hands have acted in both instances?"

Diana stared at him. "Are you putting the death of Mavis down to the ghost?"

"Pehaps. There are still the opened graves to be explained as well. These things may all be connected."

"You once said that you thought Mario's spirit had finally come to rest. And then you wondered if something had happened to change that. You should be able to tell more easily than any of us. Do you think Mario's ghost is causing this trouble?"

"I haven't decided yet," Barnabas said quietly.

She studied him with worried eyes. "I hope they don't involve you in any of this."

"I doubt that they can," he said.

They had barely finished their discussion when the

farmhouse door opened and Alex Carter came into the big room, looking distraught. He gave them a bitter glance. It was easy to see that the death of Mavis had been a hard blow for him.

Coming over to her, he asked, "Where is Norrad?"

"He's resting in one of the rooms. You shouldn't bother him."

Alex's eyes held a wild gleam of rage and he stood there seeming barely able to control himself, his hands clenching and unclenching.

"He murdered her," Carter said harshly.

"You can't be sure of that," she challenged him.

"Who else, then?" he demanded.

Barnabas said quietly. "Has the coroner discounted the possibility that she took her own life?"

Alex gave him one of his arrogant looks. "I don't care what the coroner thinks. I know that Peter Norrad threatened her life and in the end he finished her."

Diana said, "That's nonsense talk. You'll only start a scandal and probably not be able to prove anything. The future of the company will likely rest on whether she's a suicide or not."

"Do you think I care about the company now?" Carter asked, his rage choking him. And with that he turned and went back out into the night again.

She sighed. "We're bound to have more trouble with him."

"So it seems," Barnabas said. "He's more than anxious to have Peter accused of his wife's murder."

"It's just a continuation of their feud," she said wearily. "I was sure it wouldn't end. Not even with her death. And it hasn't!"

Barnabas gave her a warning look. "With tension in the company at its peak, you may be in worse danger than you know. You must be doubly careful from now on."

"This may be the end of the summer ballet," she reminded him. "It wouldn't surprise me if Elizabeth decided she didn't want us here any longer. The scandal from Mavis' death is bound to upset her."

"When I talked with her a short while ago, she was very pleased with the company being here," Barnabas said.

"That was before all this happened."

"She's a very fair woman. I doubt that she'll make any rash decisions."

Diana gave him a searching glance. "Why did you have to see her tonight? You seemed to consider it very urgent."

"I wanted to ask her whether I should leave or not," Barnabas said. "After that incident of last night I was worried."

"You didn't tell me that's what you were seeing her for."

"I preferred to wait," he said. "As it happens, she believes I should ignore the stories they are spreading about me and continue on here for a short while longer, at least."

Her eyes met his. "Does Elizabeth know the full truth about you?"

He shook his head.

"I see," Diana said. "I wanted to be certain. It's a responsibility, knowing."

"Yes," he said with a sigh. "I'm sorry you had to find out."

She touched a hand to his arm. "Don't ever feel that way. I needed to know. Now I can help you."

The farmhouse door opened again and Stefan came in, accompanied by Chief Haig. The short, stout man looked dejected.

"So we meet again, Miss Samson," he said. "And a nasty business it is that has brought us together."

"We're all shocked," she agreed.

"Another violent death at Collinwood," the police chief said. "And, I suppose, the foundation for another ghost story." He gave Barnabas one of his shrewd glances. "I guess you know more than most of us about the Collinwood ghosts, eh, Mr. Collins?"

Barnabas showed no expression on his handsome face as he replied quietly, "Yes. I suppose I do."

CHAPTER EIGHT

The first thing Elizabeth Stoddard did about the death of
Mavis Norrad was to send the children, David and Amy,
off to Vermont with Maggie Evans for a week. Diana
could well understand that the mistress of Collinwood was
anxious to remove the youngsters from the tense atmosphere for at least a short period.

Mary Wentworth was back to her usual health the
morning following the tragic incident. She returned to her
room at Collinwood and at once held a council of war
with Elizabeth and Roger. The verdict of the coroner had
been death by suicide, so the company had been spared
the worse scandal of a murder having been perpetrated.

Diana did not know exactly what had been discussed at
the meeting, but later, Carolyn told her what she had
learned from her mother.

She strolled with Diana in the garden and confided,
"Mother insisted that Miss Wentworth continue her season
here in spite of what happened to Mavis."

"I'd hoped that she would," Diana said.

The pretty teenager grimaced. "I understand Uncle
Roger put up a very strong argument. He wanted the company to leave at once, but Mother wouldn't hear of it."

"I can imagine your Uncle Roger wasn't pleased."

"He simply threw up his hands and told Mother she
could take on the full responsibility for anything that
might happen from now on. And he seemed sure that
something bad was bound to happen."

Diana smiled ruefully. "I'd expect the law of averages is
on our side. We've had so much bad luck already."

"I hope so," Carolyn agreed. "And then Uncle Roger
was also angry about Cousin Barnabas staying on. He
thinks he is causing gossip and hurting the family name."

"That's too bad."

"In a way it's true," Carolyn admitted. "Barnabas

95

wears such freaky clothes, and the way he roams around at night makes people think he's some kind of madman. That's why they blame him for those attacks on the town girls."

"I know," she said.

"At least Mavis' suicide has stopped a lot of that kind of gossip," Carolyn said. "They're too busy talking about why she did it. A lot of them don't believe it was suicide."

Diana halted and looked at the younger girl. "They don't?"

"No. The night before Mavis was found dead in the chapel a lot of people heard her husband threatening her in the Blue Whale. She was there on a date with that Alex Carter."

She sighed. "That doesn't mean he killed her. Mavis was a very unhappy woman. I think it likely she did commit suicide."

"Then some people are bringing up all that old legend about Mario Renzie and Anya Collins. And how his ghost killed her father and rang the bell in the chapel tower. They say that his ghost came back and killed Mavis and that the tower bell rang. Did you hear it?"

"I thought I did," Diana said carefully, knowing she was sure of it. "But I was very upset."

"And didn't Mary Wentworth tell everyone she saw Mavis throttled by the ghost? Mother says that's what she told her."

Diana offered a sad smile. "I think the shock of finding Mavis a suicide temporarily deranged Mary. She hasn't spoken about a ghost lately."

"I suppose she knows it is no use," Carolyn said. "She has discovered that no one believed her."

"That could be it," she admitted.

"And that's why you haven't said a lot about hearing the tower bell toll," Carolyn said.

"Chiefly because I may have imagined it," Diana said.

"What does Cousin Barnabas think about it?" Carolyn asked. "I know you two are very friendly."

Diana gave her a startled smile. "What makes you so sure of that?"

"You're always together, for one thing," the younger

girl said. "And I can tell you like each other."

"Barnabas hasn't offered any opinion yet," Diana told her. And this was quite true. He'd been very careful not to make any definite statements concerning the violent end of the ballet star's life.

"I'd like to know if he ever does say anything about it," Carolyn said. "I think he's a wonderful and smart man."

"I agree."

"I always argue on his side when anyone in the village says anything against him," Carolyn went on.

"You should."

Carolyn smiled. "You tell him that I said that."

"I will."

Carolyn gave her an admiring look. "I hear you're going to be the new star of the ballet."

"I was understudying Mavis, so I suppose I will take her place," she agreed.

"I think that's wonderful," Carolyn said. "I can hardly wait for the opening night."

"It's almost too near for most of us," Diana said truthfully. "Eleanor is just out of the hospital, and she is having to learn all my routines in the ballet."

The days and nights of preparation for *Roxanna* were about the most frantic that Diana had ever gone through. Hours of extra rehearsing for the leading role left her hardly any time to herself. In a way it was good for her. She had scant opportunity to worry about Barnabas and the horrible truth she had learned about him.

Once the ballet opened she would be able to relax, and she intended to probe then more into what had made the man she loved become a vampire and how long he had survived in this tortured state. She meant to look up everything she could on black magic and the living dead. Any obscure hint might offer her the magic key to bring Barnabas back to normalcy.

During the days of strenuous preparations for the ballet opening and the equally tiring nights, she'd seen little of Barnabas. Occasionally he would come to the chapel and sit quietly in a back row and watch her dance. She could nearly always tell when he was there. And often some of the minor performers in the company would come back and whisper of his presence in the shadowed body of the chapel.

On these occasions she would strain to make her dancing a thing of perfection so he would be proud of her. Peter Norrad made this difficult. He seemed unable to throw off the tragedy of his wife's suicide. It showed in his dancing as well as in his relationships with others in the company. There was talk that he might be on the verge of a nervous breakdown.

Often, between the times when he was onstage, he would leave the chapel and go to the old cemetery behind it and stand motionless with a bowed head among the gravestones. It was as if with the passing of Mavis he was trying to establish a communion with the dead, reaching out to those in the grave and turning his back on the living. When he returned after a session in the cemetery he was absent-minded and in a fog. Several times Diana pleaded with him to concentrate more on their dances together.

Hollowed-eyed with grief, he apologized to her as they stood together in the wings waiting for an entrance cue. "I have lost the ability to sustain a good performance. I'm sorry."

"You'd be fine if you shut out the past from your mind," she told him.

He stared at her. "You're asking me to forget Mavis and what happened to her. I can't do that."

"You must if you are to continue in your career," she warned him.

"I'm only staying on to help Mary," he said forlornly. "When I finish here I'll never set foot on a stage again."

"But Mavis wouldn't have wanted that."

"Her ghost haunts me," Peter said grimly. "She begs me to avenge her murder."

"Murder?"

He nodded. "I'm positive that's what it was."

Diana was surprised to hear him offer this opinion. The verdict of suicide had probably spared him being charged with his wife's murder, but he seemed unaware of that. Because he did, she felt that he had to be innocent. If Mavis had been murdered, someone else must be guilty.

98

"If she was murdered, have you any idea who might have done it?" she asked him.

His reply was startling.

"I think Stefan might have killed her," he said calmly. "He was strangely jealous of her and he hated her. He had an idea that she was trying to break up the company and ruin his chances to have his ballet produced."

"He wouldn't go to such lengths to stop her, would he?" she asked.

"He's a genius," Peter acknowledged. "And I've never yet known a stable genius. I believe Stefan capable of murder under the right conditions, and I think he may have staged Mavis' supposed suicide."

If Diana found dancing with Peter Norrad difficult, it was just the opposite when she was working onstage with Alex Carter. The younger male lead in the ballet seemed untouched by the loss of the woman he'd courted so avidly. He was more robust and graceful in performance, and he actually seemed to have grown in competence.

But when he had a moment alone with her he was bitter in his accusations against Peter Norrad. "How can you dance with that murderer?" he wanted to know.

She gave him a reproachful look. "I'm sure Peter had nothing to do with his wife's death."

"I suppose he told you that," Alex mocked her.

She sighed. "He's not that cruel a person."

"Have you noticed how he's behaved since that night?" Alex sneered. "He's acting like a killer with a bad case of conscience."

"I see it rather differently," she said. "To me he behaves like a grieving husband."

"You don't use your eyes," the dancer said with disdain. "You're too wrapped up in your quaint friend, Barnabas."

"I'd rather you left Barnabas out of this," she said.

His eyes searched her face. "You were the one who supposedly found Mavis first. How do we know that you and Barnabas didn't finish her off? You wanted her part in the ballet. What better way to make sure of it?"

"You're making a bad mistake," she told him angrily. "It was Mary Wentworth who found Mavis hanging there first. And Barnabas and I are not murderers."

"I don't think Mary knows what happened," he replied. "And the way people in the village talk about Barnabas, he could be any mad kind of killer."

She quickly walked away from him, seething inwardly at his cruel remarks about Barnabas. The loud-talking trouble-maker was becoming unbearable. Yet she had to work with him in the ballet and somehow get along with him in spite of her growing hatred for him.

Perhaps the most eerie of all her discussions of Mavis' death came about when she escorted Mary Wentworth to her bedroom one night after a late rehearsal. Barnabas had not put in an appearance and Diana was worried about that. Mary had seemed extremely weary when Stefan drove them back from the theater. Because the old woman looked so worn out, Diana offered to see her to her room and the offer was quickly accepted.

On reaching the room, Mary Wentworth invited her to stay for a few minutes. The old woman slumped heavily into an easy chair and waved Diana to sit opposite her. Only a tiny lamp on the bedside table supplied the room with light. In the murky atmosphere of the quiet room the old woman stared across at her.

"You are doing well, girl," Mary said. "One day you may be as famous as I was in my prime."

"I can hardly hope for that," Diana said.

The wrinkled pale face showed a faraway expression. "But you must beware of the ghost—the ghost that took Mavis from us."

"You still believe that?" she asked, a chill feeling running down her spine.

"I saw it happen," the old woman said strangely. "One moment Mavis was dancing and in the next she was hanging there strangling. The chapel is haunted. Mavis died in exactly the same fashion as that Anya. The ghost was jealous of her dancing so beautifully in that place of sadness. And you will be watched and hated by the same evil eyes."

She shook her head. "I don't want to believe that."

Mary Wentworth leaned forward, her thin hands clutching the chair arms as she warned her, "You had better believe it. The ghost will be after you next. You represent youth and beauty and the ghost cannot abide that in the chapel. You'll be the target now."

Diana stood up. "You've worked too hard, and you are very weary. Would you like me to help you prepare for bed?"

"I do not need your help," Mary Wentworth said with an unexpected strength in her contemptuous reply. "I'm neither senile nor easily fooled. And what I have told you is sober truth and for your protection."

Diana saw that it was useless to do anything other than humor the old woman. "Thank you," she said. "I must go to my own room and to bed. We have another hard day tomorrow."

Mary Wentworth sat back in her chair again and gave a dry, rasping chuckle. "None of you dare face the truth," she said. "None of you but me. It takes an old woman to have courage."

"I agree," Diana said, bidding the old woman a hasty goodnight and hurrying out of the room. It had been a difficult interlude and she was more convinced than ever that the veteran dance star was gradually sinking into senility and madness.

Only when she was directing the ballet was she normal, and this was true to a pattern of people of her age and type. Small items were beyond her coping with. And one day the dark curtain of full senility would descend on the once-famed star and leave her dragging out her days in mindless tranquility. The vision of it made Diana shudder.

But at the rehearsal the following morning Mary Wentworth was as vigorous and demanding as ever. There was no hint of the broken old woman in her bearing or remarks. It was part of the magic of her talent that she could carry on in this manner.

Eleanor had returned and was quickly shaping up in the role previously played by Diana. Only two days were left before the ballet was to have its initial performance. It appeared the scandal pertaining to the death of Mavis had roused the curiosity of the village. As a result the box office at the chapel theater had been doing a land office business. All the tickets had been sold for the first week's performances and many for the second week as well. The prospects seemed excellent.

But they all would be tense until after the first night when the critics had given their opinions on the ballet. Important dance critics were coming to the obscure village to cover the ballet for the metropolitan papers. This was partly a tribute to Mary Wentworth, but it also proved that Stefan Emmon was being taken seriously as a composer.

Eleanor seemed in perfect health again but still showed a great deal of interest in Barnabas. This troubled Diana, since she knew Barnabas had used the pretty girl as a source of the blood supply he needed so desperately from time to time. And that his only feeling for her was one of casual friendship. He regarded Eleanor as a pleasant young woman sufficiently infatuated with him to come easily under his hypnotic influence.

Since admitting his taint of the vampire to Diana, he had explained to her how he had harmlessly secured blood from a number of local young women. After winning their friendship and confidence with his undeniable charm he'd cleverly placed them under a brief hypnotic spell. That was why none of them could tell what had happened or that he was the one who'd attacked them. The police had given up trying to get from the young women evidence directly linking him to the crimes.

Eleanor had no idea that there was a romance between Diana and Barnabas, and so she was indiscreet enough to confide her own feelings about him to Diana.

"I haven't been able to talk to him alone since my return," she pouted one day. "I'm sure he's avoiding me."

This came as no surprise to Diana, since she'd especially begged Barnabas to leave the girl discreetly alone. She said, "He's probably aware you need every minute to perfect your performance."

Eleanor looked wistful. "He might at least pay a little attention to me."

Diana smiled. "Don't worry about it. I'm positive you'll hear from him after the opening."

"It's as if we'd never been friends," the dark girl said unhappily. "And we were close friends."

"He may be busy with his own work," she reminded the girl. And at the same time she considered what would be the best way to inform her that Barnabas was no longer interested in her. It was bound to be awkward. Perhaps the only way would be to have Barnabas explain it to her himself. He would do it in such a charming fashion that there could be no ill-feelings afterward.

Her own meetings with him had been strictly limited, but on the night before the opening of the ballet they arranged a rendezvous at Widows' Hill. It was better for them to meet away from the chapel now and take no chance of drawing attention to their romance.

It was a suitably foggy evening. When the others had gone to their rooms and the ancient mansion was silent except for the echo of the distant foghorn she crept down the stairs and out into the cool dampness of the night to follow the cliff path to the hill high above the rocky beach.

She had brought along a flashlight which she used as soon as she was a reasonable distance from the house. And though she rarely ventured out alone since Mavis' tragic death, she felt safe enough on this mission. After all, Barnabas was only a short distance away on Widows' Hill, waiting for her. And she needed to see him before the opening to give her confidence and relax her worries about him.

The fog came in patches. It would be heavy in one spot and light in another. At times she could see quite a distance ahead and then even the grass beneath her feet would be shrouded by the white clouds. And the thick mist swirled before the beam of her flashlight and took on fantastic shapes. Sometimes they assumed forms strangely lifelike. The cowled, bent head of a girl with a slim body took shape in the mist and she halted and gasped slightly. It had looked so much like the motionless, forlorn figure of Mavis, hanging above the stage.

But as she stared at the eerie reminder of that awful night the fog quickly moved and twisted into other formations. She stood there, her heart pounding, and felt foolish at having been so easily scared. But it was surely a night for phantoms to haunt one. The lonely pounding of the waves came to her from the beach far below the cliffs.

She quickly calculated how many yards it might be to the high point of Widows' Hill, where Barnabas had promised he'd be waiting. Perhaps a hundred yards, she decided, or a little more. Her pace quickened and she wished she were already there.

Then she was suddenly seized with the panicky feeling that she was being followed. Once the notion had crept into her brain, she could think of nothing else. At every step she took, it seemed the presence haunting her gained on her just a trifle. She forced herself to keep her eyes straight ahead to avoid betraying her fear, but she could almost feel the cold hatred of the one tracking her.

Clammy sweat broke out at her temples. Again she tried to guess how much further she had to go before she'd reach Barnabas, but fright had robbed her of her ability to reason. It was all a terrified jumble in her mind. And the urge to turn and confront the silent foe following her battled with an impulse to run wildly and try and escape whoever or whatever it was.

The thumping of her own heart was sounding loud enough in her ears to drown out everything else, and then she thought she felt the phantom touch of icy fingers on the nape of her neck. She screamed out her terror and, turned, stumbling, to shine her flashlight through the rolling clouds of fog behind her.

She saw the face! That ugly, simian face with its expression of scowling hatred! It showed briefly in the heavy mist and then was lost again. She turned and ran sobbing in what she believed was the direction of Widows' Hill. But somehow she had lost her bearings, and after a few minutes, she realized she was going away from the cliffs. She could no longer hear the pounding of the waves.

She halted in the field of tall grass, staring around indecisively. And then, hoping to elude her pursuer, she threw herself down in the damp grass and pressed herself close to the ground. She had turned off the flashlight and now she listened for the warning of approaching footsteps. An alarming thought crossed her mind! Phantoms moved with speed and silence.

She lay there for long minutes and tried to decide where she had gone wrong. It seemed to her that if she went forward from where she was, she must eventually reach the cliffs again. It would be worth a try. Her nerves were just a little more under control as she rose cautiously from her refuge in the tall grass and began to walk quickly in the direction she'd decided.

After a moment she ventured to turn on the flashlight, but it was not much assistance in the thick fog. Still she plodded on grimly across the uneven field. And then there was a welcome sound, the faint pounding of the waves. As she went further, the sound became louder. A few moments after that she had found the cliff path.

She was upset and miserable from her brief minutes in the tall grass. She hoped that she would not get a cold and be ill for the opening performance. So much depended on it. Then she recalled she'd been fearful of her very life only short minutes before and so it was ridiculous to worry about a mere cold now. The ugly face she'd seen so briefly was vividly etched in her memory. And she knew it was the same one she'd seen from the bushes on that day when unseen hands had attacked her in the chapel. Perhaps there was a mysterious ghost whose angry features took shape every so often.

But she dismissed this thought recalling that both Elizabeth and Roger had agreed that the face she'd seen had belonged to Hank, the hulking brute who had worked at Collinwood for a short time before being dismissed. They'd suggested he was still lurking on the estate. Perhaps he was, and it was his face she'd seen through the mist. If so, it offered her small comfort. There was little choice between a phantom and a mad criminal!

The beam of her flashlight caught the bench on Widows' Hill through the fog. She gave a small sigh of relief. And as she swung the flashlight in another direction it picked up the blurred figure of Barnabas in his caped coat.

"Barnabas!" she called out in joyous relief.

The broad-shouldered Englishman emerged from the fog to take her in his arms. "I began to worry that you were in some sort of trouble," he said.

"I had a bad scare," she said. And after he'd kissed her she proceeded to tell him what had happened.

"It sounds as if that Hank still might be hiding out in one of the estate buildings," Barnabas said. "He could even be somewhere in the cellars of the main house. There are places where he'd never be found."

"You speak as if you knew those cellars well," she said.

"I do," he said with a grim smile on his handsome face. "I have had to seek refuge in them more than once."

She stared up at him anxiously. "There are times when I feel I know so little about you," she said.

His eyes met hers. "The tragedy is that you've learned so much."

"No," she said. "That was meant to be. But tell me. What relation are you to the original Barnabas whose portrait is in the hallway of Collinwood?"

His smile was grim. "I doubt if you'll believe me."

"Of course I will," she insisted. "Why should you lie to me?"

"Very well," he said. "That is my portrait."

"Your portrait!" she echoed, staring at the melancholy sallow face.

"I told you that you wouldn't believe me," he reminded her.

Her eyes were fixed on him. In a whisper she said. "You are the first Barnabas?"

"Yes," he said bitterly. "The first Barnabas. The victim of Angelique's curse and the one who lost Josette's love. I've lived a dozen lives since then, so it has all become a long weary blur to me."

She was still dazed at the revelation. "But that means you must be close to two centuries old!"

"Your arithmetic is excellent," he said mockingly. "Fortunately as a vampire I haven't aged at all. I'm exactly the same age as the day the curse was placed on me. And I'll not begin to age normally again until the curse is broken and I become a human being once more."

Diana studied him with gentle eyes. "That must be soon."

"I wish I felt the same way," he warned her. "I have known discouragement too many times."

"My love will save you this time," she promised.

They stood there in the darkness wreathed in fog. She pressed close to the tall handsome man who had lived far too long and endured torment beyond what could be expected. He was a phantom, a ghostly creature of the night, and yet he held no terror for her because of her love for him.

106

His arm was around her as he warned her, "You must be careful during the opening performance tomorrow night."

"Why do you say that?" she asked.

His reply was unsettling and unexpected. "Because I'm almost sure that Mavis Norrad was murdered and you may be marked as the second victim."

CHAPTER NINE

The quiet conviction of this statement from Barnabas startled her. She stared up into his handsome face. "Why do you say that?"

He looked grave. "I can't explain any more just now, but I think you should assume that a murder has been done. And the murderer could strike again."

"But Chief Haig pronounced her death a suicide."

"It looked as if it might have been," Barnabas admitted. "But that was a clever ruse on the part of the killer."

"Then why didn't the police investigate further?"

"I believe they may be doing exactly that now."

She gave a tiny shiver as the full impact of her dilemma hit her. She said, "You're discounting the mysterious ghost theory? Remember Mary Wentworth was there first. And she still claims Mavis was killed by invisible hands."

"An old woman's muddled thinking," he said. "Whatever she saw I do not believe it was the ghost of Mario."

"Yet, Mavis was found hanging in almost the precise spot they found Anya," Diana reminded him.

"The murderer wants everyone to believe the supernatural is involved," Barnabas warned her. "And he was no doubt hiding in the back of the chapel after tolling the tower bell. You entered the chapel and trapped whoever it was. So he made his escape by brushing violently past you in the darkness."

"He almost knocked me down."

"And whoever it was is bound to worry whether you have any clue to their identity or not," Barnabas told her. "At any time you may piece together what happened and decide you know who it was. That is why the murderer will inevitably strike again and you will be his victim."

A baffled expression crossed her pretty face. "You make it sound so real," she said. "And if you're right I'm in serious trouble."

"You should be aware of your danger."

Diana frowned. "It's Peter Norrad you suspect, isn't it? He had the strongest motive for killing his wife. And he has acted strangely ever since. Even his dancing has been affected."

Barnabas shook his head. "I'm not pointing an accusing finger at anyone," he said. "When I know more I will tell you. For the moment I can only warn you to be cautious."

"That's not too easy," she said.

Barnabas gave her a fond smile. "Don't allow it to bother your performance. Remember I'll be close by tomorrow night. You won't be entirely without protection."

"I realize that," she said. "But I also worry about you. Chief Haig is suspicious of you and your reasons for keeping to yourself in the daytime."

"I know that," he said.

"You should visit his office one of these evenings and try to placate him," Diana worried. "What would happen if the police decided to force their way into the old house?"

He shrugged. "Hare would attempt to protect me as best he could."

"What match would he be against the police?"

Barnabas smiled grimly. "It would be a rather uneven contest, I'll grant you. But my hiding place in the cellar is fairly well concealed. Hare would make sure the door to the room containing my coffin was securely locked and camouflaged with packing boxes and cartons piled up before it."

"You don't think they would find you?"

"I very much doubt it," he said. "You see, they don't know what to look for. As clever as Chief Haig is, I doubt that he accepts the theory I could be a vampire."

"No," she agreed. "He probably thinks you are eccentric to the point of insanity."

Barnabas appeared satisfied. "As long as he thinks that, I'm in a relatively safe position."

"I wish I could be sure of that," she sighed.

"If the truth be told, I'm probably in less danger than you are," he said.

She studied him with anxious eyes. "But you do have to take certain risks. I know little about your condition beyond the fact you require fresh blood every so often. That means incidents like the other night and more gossip and suspicion."

He frowned. "You must not think about that. Don't concern yourself with it. I'll manage."

"What about Eleanor?" she asked. "I'm sure she is in love with you."

"I'm sorry," he said. "I had no intention of that happening."

"You must talk to her when you have a chance," Diana suggested. "Explain to her about us."

"I will," he said.

"The longer she goes on thinking of you in a romantic way, the worse the letdown will be," she said.

Barnabas made no answer to that. His gaunt, handsome face wore an expression of deep frustration as he gazed off into the swirling mist. The foghorn gave its regular doleful blast to break the silence between them.

He turned to her. "I must see you back to the house."

"I hate to go," she said. "I'll not see you again until after the opening of the ballet."

"I'll be there in the audience," he promised. "And I'll come to you backstage as soon as it is over."

Satisfied with that, she strolled back to Collinwood. He escorted her to the door and they kissed goodnight. She went inside and then watched from a ground floor window as he walked off into the fog. It took only a moment or so before he'd vanished into the gray mist.

With a feeling of sadness Diana allowed the window drape to fall in place and turned and started up the stairway. Her meeting with Barnabas had begun frantically. There had been the fears of the unknown that had assailed her as she made her way through the fog-ridden night, and these had been climaxed by her vision of that terrifying face in the ghostly haze. Her flight from this horror had left her in a state of panic by the time she'd finally found Barnabas.

Being with Elizabeth's handsome cousin nearly always gave her a feeling of warmth and security. She had come to love Barnabas in spite of knowing his dreadful secret and she was sure that he loved her in return. But tonight he had upset her with his talk of Mavis having been murdered and his insistence she could be the next victim. Yet he had given her no actual proof to back up his words.

She was supposed to accept his warning and ask no questions, but it was not easy. She still was haunted by a feeling that the supernatural was involved in all that had gone on at the chapel. She couldn't forget those graves despoiled as if the long dead had actually risen up from them. And she thought that those uneasy spirits must resent the intruders in the chapel and perhaps had sought revenge on them.

Mary Wentworth backed the theory that ghosts were responsible for Mavis' death. Invisible hands had dealt with the dancer, according to the old woman. Was Mary a little mad, or was she covering up for someone? It was something to think about.

Barnabas was allied with the phantom world. Diana must never forget that. Until some way was found to lift the curse from him, he was one of the night creatures. Despite their love, this barrier remained between them, and it was possible that he was protecting the ghost of Mario by insisting a human was responsible for murdering Mavis.

At this point Diana was thoroughly confused. She was not even sure that Mavis had been murdered. Chief Haig seemed ready enough to accept the suicide theory. But as Barnabas had made clear, the chief might at the same time still be working on the case. She wished the opening night of the ballet with its tension was over.

In her room she quickly prepared for bed. At the last moment she decided to take a warm shower to counteract the chilling she'd received in the fog. Putting on a robe, she went down to the bathroom. The shower took her only a short time and then she started back to her room.

She'd only gone a few steps when she heard the boards of the hall floor creak behind her. She turned quickly to be confronted by Alex Carter.

"You're keeping late hours," he said.

111

"Why did you come up behind me that way?" she asked angrily. "You frightened me."

He arched an eyebrow. "I thought you were completely nerveless," he said. "You prowl about the cliffs in the midnight hours. Even on a foggy night like this. And you hold secret trysts with the mad Barnabas."

She stared at him in a rage. "Do you make a hobby of spying on me?"

"I'm just guessing what might have kept you out so late the night before the opening," he teased her. "And it seems by your reaction I've guessed right."

"How clever of you!" she said bitterly and turned to go on to her room.

"Diana!" he called after her.

She paid no attention but hurried on to her door and went in and locked it after her. Alex was becoming more obnoxious all the time. She didn't know how much longer she could put up with him. She promised herself to complain to Mary Wentworth about him, fully realizing that this would do little good. The old woman seemed to think Alex could do no wrong. Reaching this frustrating conclusion, Diana slid between the sheets and turned out her light.

Sleep came with surprising rapidity. She was much more exhausted than she realized. The long rehearsal of the early evening followed by the tensions of the later hours had worn her out. Her sleep was deep and dreamless and she had no idea how long it went on, but she suddenly wakened in the darkness to a familiar but alarming sound.

From a distance she clearly heard the eerie tolling of the chapel bell. It went on for several minutes, then ended, and the foghorn was all that broke the silent darkness with its regular warnings.

Diana had come fully awake at the sound of the chapel bell. She continued to sit up in bed, wondering if anyone else had heard it. What was the legend? That whenever there was to be a death the bell tolled. And it had tolled tonight!

Was there to be another murder in the ancient chapel? And was she to be the victim? Her throat went taut with fear as she recalled the warning Barnabas had given her, and wished she had the freedom to leave Collinwood and escape from all the terrors the estate had brought her. But she owed allegiance to the others in the company whose livelihood depended on the success of the ballet. And she had Barnabas to consider. Poor doomed Barnabas!

Surely, if he could bear the curse that had shadowed him from the long ago days of the first Collinwood, she could stand up under the strain she faced now. She lay back on her pillow with a sigh and stared up into the darkness, trying to picture what lay ahead for her. She was still trying to do this when sleep gently closed her eyelids again and she sank into a second but more restless slumber.

If good weather could be considered an omen, the warm, bright day that followed should have meant the best of luck for their venture. Diana waited at breakfast for some of the others to mention hearing the chapel bell during the night, but no one spoke of it. She was forced to come to the conclusion that she was the only one who'd heard it. Or had it been part of a lingering nightmare? She thought not, since she recalled it so vividly.

Elizabeth engaged her in conversation in the hallway after breakfast. The dark-haired, attractive mistress of Collinwood smiled and asked, "Will you have any more rehearsals today?"

"No," Diana said. "We finished last night. The idea now is to relax and rest for the performance tonight."

"That sounds very sensible," Elizabeth agreed. "But it must be difficult. You all must be so excited. Your first performance and the house sold out. And the critics coming to write their reviews."

Diana smiled wistfully. "We all are pretty much on edge. The tragedy of Mavis hasn't made it easier. I'll be happy when tonight is over."

"It's a lovely day," Elizabeth said. "Why don't you go down to the beach?"

"I may," she said. "A swim and a rest under the sun might be the ideal thing."

"Just so long as you don't overdo it," the older woman warned.

The more Diana thought about the beach the more it appealed to her. She went upstairs and changed into her two-piece black bathing suit. Taking a bag with some suntan oil, a towel and a magazine, she left the house and crossed the lawns to the path leading down to the beach. There was a small sandy beach and a wharf almost directly in front of Collinwood at the foot of the cliffs. The path down was steep and she made her way along it carefully.

Reaching the sandy stretch she discovered two or three large colored beach umbrellas had been set out there. She established herself under one of them, stretching out one of her towels and placing her bag with her other things by it. Then she put on her bathing cap and went down to the water to touch a toe to the waves as they rolled in and test for temperature.

The water was cold, but she forced herself to step in until she was almost up to her knees. She soon became used to the chill. And after a few further moments of accustoming herself to the cool Maine ocean water she plunged in for a swim. She found it like a tonic, but she was careful not to go out too far. She came back and stood in shallow water before having a second swim.

Then she returned to the beach to dry herself off and rest a little. As she left the water she was surprised to find Stefan Emmon standing by her umbrella smiling at her. The young composer wore blue trunks and he had an unexpectedly muscular body. He looked more youthful and healthy in a bathing suit than he did when seated at the piano.

"Water cold enough?" he asked.

She laughed and shivered as she bent down for her towel. "Icy but wonderful," she said.

"I know," he agreed. "I go in nearly every morning."

Diana paused in her toweling to stare at him. "I had no idea you were a swimmer."

He smiled bitterly. "You don't expect me to spend all my time at a piano, do you?"

"Of course not," she said.

"Marvelous day," he went on, staring up at the sky with only a few scattered woolly clouds against the soft blue. "Should be ideal weather for the opening."

She had finished drying herself and was seated under the umbrella. She clasped her hands around her knees. Offering him a smile, she asked, "Are you nervous?"

"What do you think? With Clive Barnes coming all the way from New York to write us up."

"He isn't making the trip for us alone," she reminded him. "Isn't he stopping at Tanglewood and Ogunquit along the way for performances at both places?"

Stefan nodded. "Nevertheless he'll be in Collinsport tonight. And so will the others from Boston and Bangor. I hope they aren't too hard on poor *Roxanna*."

"They'll like the ballet," she assured him. "But I'm not so positive how he'll feel about our performances."

Stefan sat down on the towel beside her. "I hope they'll find the company up to the usual Mary Wentworth standards," he said. "And I know that even Barnes will like you."

She smiled. "That probably comes under the heading of flattery."

"I mean it," he insisted. "I thought Mavis was fine. But you've given the role more dimension. And your dancing has an exuberance she lacked. That must be hard with Peter giving such a lackluster showing."

"He isn't at his best," she agreed, her face clouding. "But that's not strange, under the circumstances."

Stefan stared out at the ocean with a troubled look on his sensitive face. "It's a weird situation," he said. "Sometimes when I look up on the stage during a rehearsal I felt that Mavis was standing there in the background watching with a mocking smile. Her presence is still that real in the chapel."

She frowned. "How odd that you should mention that," she said. "I sometimes have the same sensation when I'm doing her part—that she's standing in the shadows of the wings, watching me."

"The company is haunted by her," Stefan said, looking at her with troubled eyes. "I wonder if the critics will sense that."

"I hope not," she said. "But they can't help being influenced by the atmosphere of our theater. The old chapel is so quaint and unique. When you combine it with the woods fringing it on one side and the old cemetery on the other it is completely different."

"Yes," he agreed. "Exactly right for a ballet of a village haunted by phantoms. It appears Collinwood is the same sort of place."

"I hadn't thought of the similarity," she said.

He gave her a direct look. "You know that most people in the company still believe Mavis was murdered."

"But why should they?" she protested.

"Because the fact of suicide wasn't clear enough," he said grimly. "Peter is under suspicion by the majority. Alex has even gone so far as to accuse me of killing her. He says I was afraid she was going to break up the company and stop the ballet from being performed. And that I hated her even though she was my half-sister."

"Alex Carter is a boor and an idiot," Diana said angrily.

The composer shrugged his muscular bare shoulders. "He is anxious to avenge her death, even though she may have taken her own life. He feels he's been cheated and he wants to make somebody pay."

"It's bad enough for him to accuse Peter, but why you?"

Stefan gave her one of his grim looks. "It might not be as far-fetched as you think. I've just finished telling you I prefer you in the role. And the way Mavis was heading, there had to be a battle between Peter and Alex. They both would have left the company and we'd have had no choice but to close."

"You're making it too easy. Fitting everything to prove his wild theory."

Stefan's eyes were cold. "And I did hate Mavis," he said. "She had my mother's looks and no moral character at all. She was a disgrace to our name."

The venom in his voice shocked her. She stared at him. Then she said, "You may have despised her, but you didn't murder her. You're much too kind a person."

The coldness left his eyes and he smiled thinly. "Thanks for your vote of confidence."

"I'm sure it's merited," she said.

"The fact remains, Alex may have made some of the company think I'm a possible killer. All of us are under suspicion. Why not Alex himself? Mavis might have finally rejected him."

116

"I think not," Diana said. "I saw them together the night before her death. They were still very close. And you can eliminate Eleanor, since she was in the hospital when it happened."

Stefan gave her a wise look. "You're forgetting another prime suspect. The one who first discovered the body and whom you found in the chapel. Mary Wentworth."

Diana was astonished. "Why should she kill Mavis, assuming she had the strength to do it?"

"The strength of madness cannot be measured even in as frail a person as Mary Wentworth," the composer said. "And if you're looking for a motive, why not insane jealousy? Mavis was always making cutting remarks to Mary Wentworth about her age and infirmity. I'm sure the old woman resented them, though she took them placidly enough. In a fit of insanity she might have decided to destroy Mavis and then collapsed from the effort afterward."

She listened with a growing feeling of incredulous fear. "It's a bizarre thought," she said. "And Mary Wentworth has talked rather madly about a ghost causing the death of Mavis. She began that as soon as she regained consciousness."

Stefan smiled. "So you see. Even the most elderly and infirm can be included in our list of suspects."

Diana shook her head. "I won't listen to you any more. It's unhealthy. I'm sure Mavis was a suicide."

Stefan spread a hand in a resigned gesture. "I think about that quotation that says the lady doth protest too much. It could have been you. I'll bet some of the company wonder about that."

"Me!"

"Sure. You claim someone was tolling the bell in the chapel when you got there. But no one else seems to have heard the bell. And your story that someone brushed past you in the darkness and escaped without your seeing them is your story alone. You haven't any other witnesses."

She frowned. "Whoever it was pushed me aside so roughly I was almost knocked down."

"I believe you," he said, mocking eyes fixed on her. "But if you did have such a close brush with the murderer, why hasn't he come back to try and eliminate you. You present a danger in that you may later decide you know who it was."

His reasoning was so close to that of Barnabas' that she was amazed. She gave him a sharp glance. "It's funny, but someone else said almost that same thing to me."

"Barnabas Collins?"

"Why do you think of him?"

He shrugged again. "He's the logical one to think of. Everyone knows you spend a lot of time in his company."

"I wasn't aware of the interest in me."

"You are our leading dancer now," he said.

"I hadn't expected to pay a price of privacy for the privilege," she said with a bitter smile.

"You should have. And while we're on the subject, what is the particular attraction of Barnabas for you?"

"I like him. Isn't that enough?"

"That's always enough," he agreed. "But I find your liking for him difficult to understand. He's not the most popular person here at Collinwood."

"What has that to do with it?"

Stefan stared out at the ocean again. "I have it on pretty sound information that Roger Collins wants him off the property. And he doesn't ever want him to return. He blames him for the attacks that have been made on those village girls."

Diana was upset to hear Stefan discussing Barnabas with such cold objectivity. And she worried that it might be deliberate. Stefan might be baiting her to divulge any secret facts she might have discovered about the man she loved. She knew she must be wary.

She said, "As far as I know, there have been no direct links between Barnabas and those attacks."

"He was seen in the village on the nights they were made. And several times he was in the company of girls who were later attacked."

"That doesn't prove anything. Probably a lot of other men were also seen in their company."

Stefan gazed at her evenly. "But the man they suspect is not just any normal person. The police believe he must be a recluse with a taint of madness. That he must be obsessed with the idea he is a vampire. The marks of teeth on the throats of those girls bear them out."

118

"Barnabas is a cultured gentleman," she told him. "I've seen no hint of insanity in him."

The composer said, "I know you're bound to defend him. And probably he shows his best side to you. But he could be two individuals. The danger is that one day those two individuals might merge into a single insane one and you'd find yourself linked to a madman."

"I can't go along with that," she protested.

"You're deliberately closing your eyes to truth," he told her. "Don't you think it odd that Barnabas lives alone in that old house and never shows himself in daylight?"

"He is busy working in the days."

"His story!" Stefan said with disdain. "And what about that mute servant, Hare? He's right out of some kind of horror story. And in the daytimes he guards the house like a watchdog."

"How can you discredit a man for having a devoted servant?"

"And the clothes this Barnabas Collins wears," the young man went on. "Whether the night is warm or cold he always has on the same caped coat. And it is Victorian in style."

"Many Londoners wear clothes like his," she said. "Our own hippies wear clothes of ancient style."

"Barnabas Collins is not a hippie," Stefan told her. "I'm only asking you to face facts."

"And why are you so concerned?"

The young man's face flushed. "Do I have to tell you?"

"I think so. Since you've gone this far."

"Very well," Stefan said very quietly. "I'm concerned because I happen to be in love with you myself."

And before she could make any reply he had come closer to her and taken her in his arms. His kiss was as warm as it was unexpected, and when he let her go, there was a resigned smile on his face.

"Sorry," he said. "I meant to wait until tonight. But I thought better of it when I realized you'd surely be with him after the performance."

He got up and walked away from her, and she watch as he climbed the path up the cliff and vanished. whole episode had been completely a surprise.

The revelation that he was in love with her wa

119

enough. But he had also presented her with another perplexing and even terrifying possibility when he suggested that Barnabas might be insane. She'd accepted the word of the handsome Englishman that he was a vampire. It amazed her that she'd done so without any kind of proof. It was an incredible story. Perhaps a madman's story!

CHAPTER TEN

The opening night of the Mary Wentworth Ballet was perhaps the most exciting event at Collinwood in years. Elizabeth Stoddard hosted a special dinner for the principals staying at the house and Roger Collins presided at the dinner table, looking grumpy in a tuxedo.

Spotlights had been mounted in trees facing the ancient chapel to provide illumination for the patrons and give a suitable touch to the rustic quaintness of the setting. A nearby field had been staked out as a parking area with two men on duty at performance time.

The problem of dressing rooms for the members of the ensemble had been solved when Mary Wentworth had rented two large trailers from a local automobile dealer and had them set out at the rear of the chapel. This left the small dressing rooms erected backstage to be used by Diana and the other stars of the ballet troupe.

Diana's tiny cubicle was at the rear right corner backstage and near the door leading outside. As time for the curtain approached, she forgot all else to concentrate on her performance. There were several changes of costume required of her and a change of make-up in the second act when she appeared first as a hag and later reverted to a young girl again. She hoped to accomplish most of this with a few deft lines and her posture, but it all took planning.

Mary Wentworth, in black evening gown, remained out front to greet the visiting critics and notables before coming backstage to see the performance begun. She seemed tiny and frail as she bobbed about in the shadows to check on all the details. One of the final things she did was to drop by Diana's dressing room.

"This is your big night, my dear," the old woman said. "Don't fail us."

The next one to visit her was Stefan. She had n

with the young composer since their strange conversation on the beach that morning—the conversation that had ended with his kissing her. He knocked gently on her door, and when she opened it, stood there in his tuxedo and black tie, looking slightly embarrassed.

"I wanted to wish you luck," he said. "I hope you don't mind."

She smiled. "Of course not. Thank you."

He hesitated. "About this morning. I didn't mean to upset you."

"It was all right," she said.

"I meant everything I said," he told her. And with a nod he left.

She blushed as she shut the door again. She couldn't easily forget that he'd said he was in love with her. And then there had been all his insinuations about Barnabas. She preferred to put them out of her mind for the time being.

When she'd first met Stefan she'd felt he was sullen and neurotic. Now she was more apt to term him shy and sensitive. She knew him a lot better, and with this knowledge had come an understanding of a complex character. His musical talent amounted to genius. She was almost certain his ballet would be praised whether the performance was liked or not.

Then she heard him playing the overture on the other side of the curtain. And she knew the minutes would pass quickly and she would soon be joining the rest of the company onstage for the opening group dance. Somebody knocked on her door and called, "Places."

She gave a final look in the small mirror with its frame of light bulbs. She seemed to be ready for her first appearance. Her heart pounding excitedly, she left the dressing room and took her place in the shadowed wings waiting for her entrance cue.

Alex Carter, beside her in his peasant outfit, smiled at her. "Don't let success go to your head," he said mockingly.

Diana turned her back on him, and then her cue came to enter and the ballet had begun for the evening. After that it was a breathless experience, and she was able to remember little of it. Painstaking rehearsal and craft took

122

over where thinking was cut off. She knew every minute detail of her role and the technique of the dancing required.

When the first curtain came after the first act, she was conscious of a tumult of applause from the small auditorium of the chapel. Afterward there was animated conversation and stirring as the patrons moved around in the building or went outside for some fresh air.

She rushed back to her dressing room to make her first major switch of costume and to line her pretty face for the scene in which she returned as a crone. She felt the ballet was going well and had received rushed congratulations from others in the show. But it was hard to know.

Barely had she gotten ready for the second act when the call for places was given again. From there on, the moments sped by. Peter Norrad's dancing improved from rehearsal and Alex Carter was at least competent. Eleanor, in the supporting role she had, received much applause for her solo number.

Then the ballet ended and they took their bows. The applause was impressive, and smiling down in the darkness of the auditorium, Diana hoped that the people had liked it all that much.

Mary Wentworth was the first to come around backstage with Elizabeth at her side. "It was a star performance," the white-haired director of the troupe said with tears brimming in her eyes. "The critics liked it. I could tell."

Elizabeth shook hands with her and smilingly said, "I was thrilled and so were all the others. Even Roger enjoyed himself."

Others milled around her with congratulations until she was exhausted. At last Barnabas was standing before her with a smile on his handsome face.

"I have seen all the great ones," he said. "And the performance you gave here tonight on this small stage made me proud of you." He kissed her.

It was the peak of her evening. "Thanks," she whispered. "I'm so weary."

He nodded. "You must be. Shall I wait for you or would you prefer to go straight home and rest?"

"Please wait," she begged. "We can talk if only for a few minutes. I'm so relieved to have this over with."

"There are performances every night from now on," Barnabas reminded her.

"They don't matter," she said. "Tonight was the challenge."

"I'll wait for you at the entrance," Barnabas told her. And he left her to make his way through the backstage groups, a tall heroic figure in his caped coat and with his silver-headed cane.

She stood there for a minute and from the corner of her eye saw that Stefan was standing a distance away and had been watching her and Barnabas talk. Then he came over to her.

"You were fabulous," he said, touching his lips lightly to her cheek. "I'm sure we were a success. There's to be a party for the company at the farmhouse. Everyone is attending except Peter. He's vanished somewhere. Will you come?"

She shook her head. "I'm really awfully tired. Make my excuses. Some other night."

Stefan had stiffened. "Of course," he said in an almost curt tone. "You will want to spend the rest of this important evening with your friend."

Diana raised her eyebrows. "Barnabas is seeing me back to Collinwood," she admitted, resenting his change of manner and his evident jealousy.

"That doesn't surprise me," he said, and with a bow, left her.

She was upset by the incident and hurriedly returned to her dressing room. In the scant privacy it offered her she slowly changed her clothes and removed her make-up. As she worked before the small mirror she thought of Stefan's behavior and felt a kind of desolation.

Her weariness literally drenched her, and with the performance over, she realized more clearly than ever that the ghost of Mavis had truly been onstage all evening. She had created the role with the memory of Mavis playing it in her mind. And the others in the cast must have had at least momentary visions of the dead girl dancing gaily to the strains of that wonderful waltz whose haunting melody would always be identified with the ballet.

Difficult as the evening had been for her, it must have been more trying for Peter Norrad. She wondered where he had gone. And she felt anger at Stefan for being so cold in his denunciation of Barnabas Collins. His scathing comments about Elizabeth's handsome cousin had even made her doubt him for a short time.

Then she saw that she had been wrong. Stefan had merely been trying to pry information from her, and she congratulated herself that she had told him nothing. The courtly man waiting for her now at the entrance to the chapel was certainly not insane. She could never be made to believe that. It didn't matter what others might think. She knew better.

She would rather have him a tortured victim of a curse, one of the walking dead, than the madman pictured by Stefan. Having managed to open in the ballet, she would have more time to devote to Barnabas. She was sure a way could be found to cure him and release him from the coffin that had been his daily refuge for so long.

Because of her troubled thoughts, she'd taken longer in changing than the others. The backstage area seemed to have emptied. She heard no voices or any sounds of movement outside her dressing room, and she worried that she had kept Barnabas waiting too long as she rose from her make-up table. It would be good to spend a short time with the man she loved and then return to Collinwood for the rest she needed so badly.

Snapping off the lights in her dressing room, she emerged into the shadowed area of backstage. It was empty of people now and the stage lights had been turned off except for the single night light that was always left in the center of the stage. Again she was seized by thoughts of Mavis, and of how she'd come upon her body dangling over the stage that awful night.

A stirring of fear welled within her and she began to walk across the dark area to the exit that led to the body of the chapel and the front entrance. All the phantoms that had ever plagued the ancient building seemed to be hovering around her now. She could almost feel the coldness of their shrouds and the lost whisperings of their clamoring voices. She knew there were such things as ghosts, and finding her alone and weak in this rendezvous of theirs they had chosen to torment her.

Her footsteps became quicker as she fairly ran for the

door lost in the shadows, but before she could reach it, invisible hands caught her and in a moment were crushing her throat. She uttered an agonized moan as she attempted to fight them off, but it was a futile effort and the mad throttling continued until she meekly closed her eyes and became limp.

She was on the floor and Barnabas was bending over her. "What happened?" he demanded anxiously. "Did you faint?"

She stirred and gave a small moan. "Something came after me. Tried to choke me."

He quickly assisted her to her feet. "I worried that you were so long. I came back to find out why and you were stretched out on the floor."

"I was on my way to you when it happened," she said. Her throat ached and she touched it with her fingers.

"Backstage was deserted except for you," Barnabas said.

She gave him a meaningful glance. "Is it likely you'd see a ghost?"

Barnabas stared at her. "You're willing to believe it was Mario's ghost?"

"Yes," she nodded. "I had a terrible feeling of fear just before it happened. I heard nothing and saw no one, but the hands gripped me and I couldn't free myself from them."

"I warned you something like this might happen," Barnabas said. "I say it was Mavis' murderer come back to finish with you."

Her hand was pressed to her throat as she stared about her at the shadows. "Take me back to Collinwood," she said. "I'll never stay alone here at night again."

And so the evening that had begun in triumph ended on a dismal note. She was weak and ill from her ordeal, so little was said between her and Barnabas during the walk to the great mansion on the cliffs. There was a restrained sadness in his manner as he kissed her goodnight.

She slept the sleep of the totally exhausted. When she awoke, the sun was blazing in through her windows, and she saw that it was nearly noon. She took a shower and dressed and then went downstairs.

Maggie Evans was in the hall and greeted her with

sparkling eyes. "We were all thrilled by the ballet," the girl said. "And the Bangor paper says that everyone in the area should take the opportunity to see it. I'm so glad we were able to be here."

"I'm glad it went well," Diana said.

She talked to the girl a few minutes and then went out into the garden. There she found Peter Norrad standing alone, staring grimly at the distant ocean. When he heard her approach on the gravel walk he turned to her.

She said, "I missed you last night."

"I didn't stay after the performance," he said brusquely.

"I understand," she said sympathetically. "It had to be a difficult evening for you."

His eyes met hers with piercing directness and she almost winced before their angry glitter. For the first time she began to worry that the torment he had known might have unhinged his mind.

"She was there, you know," he said.

Diana nodded. "I know what you mean. We all thought of her. Remembered her in the part."

"No," he said, his tone sharp. "She was there!"

She frowned. "I don't understand."

He took a step towards her, his haggard face distorted by grief. "Every move you made, she was there behind you. When I danced with you I was dancing with two people."

"You shouldn't upset yourself about it," she said, trying to placate him.

"I could see her plainly," he maintained, not even listening to her.

"You were excellent last night," she said, hoping this would get him off the subject of Mavis.

"I always danced well with her," he said.

"Evidently the local papers were enthusiastic," she went on. "I hope the New York papers are as kind."

"I left early," he said. "I couldn't face meeting a lot of people after the performance."

"Of course not."

"But she was still there. I could see her in the shadows. She was waiting there in the shadows as I left."

Diana could see that the strain and grief Peter Norrad had known had left him in a confused state. He was

127

unable to carry on a normal conversation. The thought came to trouble her that it could be guilty conscience and not mere grief that had put him in this state. Peter could have been his wife's murderer.

He stared at her strangely for a long moment, then turned and walked quickly towards the rear of the big mansion. Watching as he vanished around the corner of the house, she felt her suspicions of him increasing. As Stefan had pointed out, Peter was the most likely suspect.

His fantasy of seeing his wife as a phantom star of the ballet was a chilling one. And his picture of the ghostly Mavis waiting in the shadows as he left the theater had also sent an icy feeling of terror through her. She began to wonder if it had been the ghost of Mavis that had attacked her in a jealous rage. And she realized how quickly this weirdness was communicated to others. She found herself standing in the warm sunlight trembling.

"There you are," a cheery voice said.

She turned to see Eleanor. The dark-haired girl was very welcome. Diana managed a smile and said, "I see you survived opening night very well."

"And the party afterward," Eleanor declared proudly. "You should have come. We had a wonderful time."

"I didn't feel up to it."

"Everyone showed up but you and Peter," the other girl said. "Even Mary stayed for a short time. Then I believe Roger Collins drove her and Elizabeth home."

"I came straight back here," Diana said. She was tempted to tell Eleanor of her eerie brush with death backstage but decided against it. She doubted that Eleanor would believe her, and it seemed wise not to say too much about it at the moment.

"Barnabas was at the party for a while," Eleanor said with a knowing smile.

This came as a shock to her. She hadn't dreamed of Barnabas returning to the farmhouse and the revelry. Then she recalled that he had behaved in an oddly restrained manner when they'd said goodnight. Had he been torn by the urge for blood?

Trying to appear casual about the unexpected information, she asked, "Did you have a chance to talk with him?"

128

"A little," Eleanor said. "Not as long as I would have liked to. He was so popular with everyone. You know he has seen all the famous stars. You should hear him describe Fonteyn and Nureyev in 'Giselle'. And he knows them personally. And he's a friend of the director of the Royal Ballet."

"It seems Barnabas was the star of your party."

"In a way he was," Eleanor said in a tone of mild surprise. "I hadn't thought about that before. All the time he was there he had a circle of the younger dancers around him."

"Mostly the girls, I'd imagine," Diana said dryly.

Eleanor laughed. "That's true. He seemed to hit it off very well with Nora. You know the cute little blonde girl."

"Yes," she said. "I've noticed her. She's new with the company."

"Talented, young and enthusiastic," Eleanor declared. "I think that is why Barnabas was attracted to her. Of course I didn't mind. I mean I wasn't jealous of her. She's much too young and unsophisticated. But I think he did enjoy telling her about Covent Garden and the Royal Ballet."

"No doubt," she said. She realized that Barnabas had not had any opportunity to talk to Eleanor and explain that he wasn't romantically interested in her. At least he hadn't done so. And he'd directed all his hypnotic charm to the winning of Nora. She couldn't help being curious about whether he and the blonde girl had met later, and if Nora had awakened in a dazed and weakened state with a certain crimson mark on her slender throat.

"I came back here with Stefan," Eleanor went on. "He seemed in a grim mood, considering how well his ballet went. I sometimes think he's seriously neurotic."

"He's not easy to understand," Diana agreed, but her thoughts were of Barnabas rather than of the young composer. "When did Barnabas leave?"

Eleanor looked surprised. "I really can't say. One moment he was there and then when I looked for him again he had gone."

Again very casually, Diana asked, "And what about all his girlfriends? Who did Nora pair off with for the evening?"

"I don't know," Eleanor said. "I didn't pay too much attention to her other than notice she'd been talking to Barnabas. I suddenly found myself tired and when Stefan offered to take me home I went with him."

The reply was entirely unsatisfactory as far as Diana was concerned, though she'd expected it would be something like that. And she was even more convinced that Barnabas had chosen Nora as his victim for last night. She decided to find out the truth somehow.

Luncheon was served on the terrace at Collinwood. It was a happy occasion, for the New York papers had arrived and the reviews were good. Mary Wentworth had other encouraging news.

The old woman smiled at Diana across the table and told her, "The New York City Ballet director phoned me long distance about an hour ago. They're interested in using *"Roxanna"* for their spring season and they asked about you as a possible member of their group."

Diana was thrilled at the news but experienced enough in the field to know that such early enthusiasm often vanished. Later the New York director might have second thoughts and hesitate in following through. She said, "I'd like to see our own company continue to use *Roxanna*."

Mary Wentworth nodded. "And so we will. But I wouldn't want to hold Stefan back from a chance to have his work produced at the New York State Theater."

Stefan, seated beside Mary, smiled and said, "We can worry about that when a definite contract comes."

Elizabeth, at the head of the table, was still in a radiant mood induced by the experience of the opening night. She said, "I thought the whole thing was marvelous. The chapel looked so picturesque under the spotlighting, and the audience was elegantly dressed. And everything on the stage seemed perfect to me. You've all worked so hard you deserve this success."

Alex Carter had been silent at his place. With a slight sneer on his face, he said, "Too bad Mavis didn't live to share our glory."

There was a sudden hush at the table. The statement had a grim effect on them all, but it seemed to upset Peter Norrad more than any of them. He gave Carter an angry look, tossed his napkin on the table, and left the table abruptly.

No one made any direct comment on his leaving, but the happy magic of the occasion had been ruthlessly shattered by the arrogant young dancer who had courted Mavis so shamelessly with no thought of her husband. Diana suddenly realized that most of the newspaper accounts had given scant mention to the dancing of Alex Carter. He had not caught the attention of the critics. No doubt this helped explain his sullen mood.

None of them lingered at the table once the mood was broken, and Diana separated herself from the others and went up to her room. She was in a strange frame of mind. At a moment when she should have been occupied by thoughts of her own success, she was concerned about Barnabas and what he had done the night before.

So strong was her curiosity that she knew she must satisfy it, and that meant going over to the farmhouse where the youngsters of the ensemble lived. She rarely went there but they would no doubt welcome her on the day after the opening. If she was lucky she would see Nora. A glance at the girl's throat would tell her whether she'd been with Barnabas or not.

She waited until the house quieted some. Then around three o'clock she made her way downstairs. She quickly headed along the lane leading to the chapel and the farmhouse. The day was lazy warm. She knew she should be resting for the performance that evening, but she couldn't relax without making this visit. She passed the field where the cars had been parked and saw the grass that had been pressed down and trampled. And a few people had driven up before the chapel and left their cars to stand in line for tickets.

She went by them and no one recognized her in her dark glasses, shorts and blouse. As she drew near the farmhouse she saw the girls and boys sprawled out on the lawn around it, sunning themselves.

Reaching the door of the farmhouse, she was greeted by Tom, one of the ensemble. He smiled at her and said, "You've arrived late for the party."

She picked up his joke. "I thought it would last at least this long."

131

"It almost did," the curly-haired young man in bathing trunks declared. "Some of the gang stayed right up for breakfast."

"I hope there won't be any heavy heads and lead feet onstage tonight," she said.

"I wouldn't want to take any bets," Tom said with a wink.

She glanced around at the couples stretched out on the grass. "Is Nora anywhere handy?"

"Nora?" The young man considered, then he pointed to a distant tree. "She's over there by herself. She's one of the gang with a monster head."

"I want to talk to her," Diana said.

She left him and walked over to the great elm under which the slim figure of Nora was sprawled on a blanket. The girl was resting on her stomach and wore a scant white bikini which emphasized her tanned lithe body. She made no move as Diana came up to her.

"Nora," she said tenatively.

The girl groaned without moving.

"It's Diana Samson," she informed the girl. "I hear you had a wonderful party last night."

Nora groaned again. "My head aches."

"I'm afraid that's the sequel to most wonderful parties," Diana said lightly.

"I never have hangovers!" the girl on the blanket protested.

"You have this time."

"I don't know why," Nora complained without lifting her head. "I had hardly anything to drink."

Diana was determined to lead her on, to make her tell more about what had happened. "Probably there was a lot of smoking and loud talk."

"I talked with Barnabas Collins," Nora said. "But it wasn't loud talk. He's very nice and he knows everything about ballet."

She continued to stand by the girl and waited impatiently for her to move. If she turned her head it would be easy to inspect her neck. Diana said, "Barnabas is a charming man."

"Yes," Nora agreed. "Old but nice." She made an attempt to lift her head and then gave up with a groan.

132

Disappointed and edgy, Diana said, "You shouldn't have stayed in the smoke and heat. You'd have been wiser to take a stroll with him outside."

"We did."

"Oh?" Diana said and hoped the sharpness of her tone had been lost on the girl.

"Yes. Barnabas suggested it. I met him out here and we talked for ages. I can't remember how long. I know that when I came back I had this awful headache and everything was a jumble."

"You don't remember when you said goodnight to him?"

"No," Nora said gloomily. "It's too bad. I liked him. I must have sort of gone blank."

"That happens," Diana said in a dry voice.

"It hasn't happened to me before," Nora said, making a move to sit up. This time she managed it, and as she sat there looking miserable, Diana was able to recognize the telltale red mark on her throat!

CHAPTER ELEVEN

Her curiosity satisfied, Diana had little interest in the girl. She knew that Nora meant nothing to Barnabas in a romantic way. She stood there in silence for a moment under the cooling shadow of the giant elm. In a few minutes she would excuse herself and go back to Collinwood.

The girl on the blanket looked up at her with wonder. "You hardly ever come here, do you?"

"No."

"You weren't here last night."

"No. I was too tired to attend the party."

Nora's pretty face showed a frown. "Aren't you a close friend of Barnabas?"

She suddenly found herself in an awkward spot. "I know him very well," she admitted.

Nora struggled to her feet and smoothed out her bikini. "Now I remember. All the girls in the company were talking about him being your fellow. Gee, I'm sorry if I did something wrong last night. I wasn't really flirting with him or anything like that. We just talked."

Diana forced a smile. "You needn't apologize. I'm sure Barnabas enjoyed your company. And since I wasn't there I can hardly complain. In fact, I don't mind at all."

"Thanks, Miss Samson," the girl said gratefully.

She said, "I notice you have a red mark on your throat. It looks like some kind of bite."

"I saw it this morning," the girl complained. "I don't know how it got there. It sort of itches. But I'll be able to cover it with make-up for tonight. It's nothing to worry about."

"No," Diana agreed with a tinge of irony in her voice. "I'm sure it isn't."

She left Nora and strolled back in the direction of the chapel. The remote old stone building no longer seemed isolated. People were driving in on the rear road continuously to order tickets. Several cars were parked outside the chapel and the line was about the same length as before.

Diana was pleased to see the interest in the project. It meant that Elizabeth Stoddard's generous gesture had been justified and the company would undoubtedly be able to pay its bills. The unhappy side of it was the mysterious death of Mavis and the tragedy it had brought them all. Not to mention her own problem of having fallen in love with Barnabas.

While she had no jealousy of the girls he cultivated because of his thirst for blood she was concerned about how long he could prey on young women of the countryside without the authorities catching up with him. If that happened, there was no telling what his fate would be. He had been very certain that Hare could protect him but she doubted it.

Somehow she must buy him time so they could try to find some cure for his unhappy condition. Why couldn't she offer her own blood to him? This should solve the problem. As far as she was concerned it need be no more weakening than a series of blood donations under regular conditions. Some people she knew offered their blood to the hospital blood banks regularly. And she needn't ever know what was happening. Barnabas could hypnotize her as he did the others. She decided to suggest this to him when she saw him again. She couldn't bear to have him at the mercy of strangers.

As she passed the chapel, some impulse made her walk over to the old cemetery rather than head back to Collinwood. When she reached the tiny area of ancient gravestones, she was amazed to discover a familiar figure there—Police Chief Joshua Haig of Ellsworth!

Haig stood there amid the wasteland of weathered tombstones. On seeing her, he came slowly over to where she had halted. It was at the spot where the graves of Mario Renzie and Anya Collins were side by side.

He tipped his hat and there was a look of interest on his face.

"You still come here regular, miss?"

"No. Not since the day you suggested I shouldn't."

He nodded. "Still, there's no danger now," he said. He

indicated the chapel. "Been a steady flow of ticket buyers here ever since I arrived."

"It does make a difference," she admitted.

His shrewd eyes were appraising her. "Your show is a hit."

"Yes."

"Me and my missus were here last night," he went on.

"I didn't know."

He spread his hands in a gesture of humility. "There wasn't any brass band to announce us in that important audience. We're just ordinary country folk."

"You've been very kind to all of us," Diana protested. "You should have come backstage. We'd have been glad to see you."

"There was a parcel of folk doin' that," he said. "Missus and me were in a hurry to get back to Ellsworth. I don't much like driving after dark. I used to be on highway patrol. Got enough of that then."

"I suppose so," she said.

"You were good in the show," the chief said watching her closely. "I understand you danced the part that girl who committed suicide was supposed to do."

"Yes," she said faintly, wondering why he was there and what this all might be adding up to.

His sharp eyes were still boring into her under the cover of the straw hat's floppy brim. "What happened to her gave you a good break."

"I would have been glad if she'd lived. I had a fine supporting role."

"That's the generous way to look at it," he agreed.

"I think we all were shadowed by the tragedy of what happened to Mavis in our performances last night."

Chief Haig's plain face registered interest. "Is that a fact?"

"I suppose in a way that is why you came," she pointed out.

"Yep," he agreed with a nod. "'If I hadn't been down here to look into her suicide I guess I wouldn't have paid much attention to your ballet at all. Never been to one before. But I thought it was pretty good."

She said, "I must get back to the house for a rest."

"Good idea," he said. He nodded towards the graves of

136

Mario and Anya. "You still take an interest in those two?"

"In a way. The legend fascinates me."

"The legend of the mysterious ghost. A lot of people around here believe in it. They claim Mario still comes back lookin' for revenge on the Collins family."

"I wonder."

"So do I," he admitted. "I've seen a heap of strange things in my time. Guess I could accept the fact of ghosts if I had enough proof. Finding the graves all dug up gave me quite a start."

"I was upset by that too."

He gave her a knowing look. "What would you think if I told you it's still going on?"

A stab of fear shot through her. "I don't know."

"Come with me," he said and turned and walked back to where he had been standing when she'd arrived. She followed him, picking her way between the green mounds marking the graves. In a moment she was at his side and she saw what he meant. Another grave had been despoiled in the same manner as the others. Earth was heaped carelessly around it and the grave was open.

She frowned. "That's horrible!"

"Never could feel much sympathy for grave robbers," Chief Haig said slowly. "Fact is, the one responsible for this must be plain crazy. No reason to it. This grave belonged to an old woman named Abigail Collins who died about two hundred years ago. I don't calculate she had many diamond rings or gold bracelets buried with her."

"Then why should anyone want to do this?"

"Crazy! Must be that," he said. He gave her another of his shrewd looks, "I have heard that your friend Barnabas Collins takes a fancy to cemeteries. Folks say he roams around in them at night like a kind of graveyard ghoul!"

She felt a surge of alarm. "Barnabas wouldn't do anything like this."

"If he's crazy enough to show himself only at night and then wanders around in cemeteries he might be just crazy enough to dig up graves."

"The stories about Barnabas are exaggerated," she protested. "People here don't understand him. Because he's

137

different, they think they have to tag him as crazy."

Chief Haig studied her. "You think you understand him better?"

"At least I'm not narrow-minded in my opinion of him."

"Well," he sighed, "I suppose we Maine folks are sort of narrow in lots of ways. But I don't know anyone native to here who would do a thing like this." And he eyed the open grave again in disgust.

She saw she had annoyed him and tried to repair the damage at once. "I didn't mean to imply the people here are ignorant. It's just that they aren't exposed to people like those of us in the cities. They don't see the way-out types."

"We've been gettin' some lately," he said. "Hippie colony down at Bar Harbor." He paused. "You been havin' any strange experiences since we talked?"

She hesitated, knowing that she had to be careful. She in no way wanted to implicate Barnabas, but some odd things had happened and she might be wise to tell the friendly police chief about them.

She said, "The other night I saw that face again, the ugly face Roger Collins believed belonged to the man called Hank."

"Where?"

"On the cliffs. It was very foggy. I had a flashlight. For just a minute his face showed in its beam. Then he vanished. I think he'd been following me."

Chief Haig frowned. "You should have phoned that information in to me."

"I didn't think it was that important. I mean, since you're keeping an eye out for him anyway."

"Any information is important," he said. "What else?"

She thought. Then she said, "One night I was wakened by the bell in the chapel tower tolling. But no one else seemed to have heard it."

"The ghost of Mario is supposed to do that," he observed dryly. "I guess you still have that ghost on your mind."

"I believe I have reason to."

"Why?"

"Last night after the show I was late leaving my dress-

138

ing room. I was very weary. As I walked towards the exit I realized I was alone in the chapel, and I suddenly felt a fear of the unknown. I was sure some phantom was there with me. In the next moment I was seized by the throat and left unconscious on the floor. Then someone came and found me."

"Who?"

Diana faltered in making a reply. She had planned not to implicate Barnabas and now he was being dragged into it. She knew there was no use lying. She said, "Barnabas Collins."

"Hmmph! I might have known he'd be in on it."

"He had nothing to do with it," she protested. "He was waiting for me outside, and when I was a long time getting there he decided to come in and see what was wrong."

The chief looked disgusted. "So you want to blame the ghost of Mario for almost strangling you?"

"It seems the most likely explanation."

"It don't seem any explanation to me at all," Chief Haig snapped.

"The chapel is haunted. Everyone around here agrees to that. Just as all of Collinwood is the scene of weird happenings."

"There are some weird happenings that cry out to be explained," the chief told her. "You should have gotten in touch with me every time you had something like this take place."

"I didn't want to bother you," she said.

"That would have been helping me," he told her. "I got a good mind to send a man out here just to keep guard on you."

"That's ridiculous," she protested.

"I'm not so sure. Looks to me like the same thing could happen to you that happened to Mavis Norrad."

"Why?"

"Maybe you know too much," he said. "Somebody is afraid of you and what you could tell."

She recalled her discovering the body of Mavis and the unknown who had rushed past her. The unknown who might have murdered Mavis and be the key to the mystery.

She said, "You called her death a suicide."

"I still haven't ruled out murder in my own mind," the chief told her. "But you need proof. And if everyone cooperates with me like you do I'm never going to wind up with anything."

"I'm sorry," she said sincerely.

He gave a deep sigh. "You may as well know that the one I got my eye on is Barnabas Collins. And my advice to you is to steer clear of him. I'd say he was crazy. He's got some kind of vampire complex that makes him attack young women and maybe dig up graves. And he's very liable to be the one who strangled Mavis and made it look like she hung herself. And now he's worryin' that you know about it and is ready to strangle you."

She listened to the chief with mounting fear. The way he told it you'd think it was true. Barnabas was so vulnerable. The truth about him was so unbelievable that it was deadly easy to build a case against him. And she could see that the loop of suspicion was gradually tightening around him.

Weakly she said, "You're making a big mistake."

"We'll see," he said shortly. "I want to hear from you the minute anything else out of the way happens."

"I'll phone you," she promised.

"See that you do," he said. "That's a police order. I won't keep you any longer. You look pretty shaky to me for a girl who has to act on stage tonight."

"I'll be all right if I get an hour's rest," she said.

Saying goodbye to him, she left the cemetery, and began the walk back to Collinwood in a frantic state of mind. It seemed almost certain the chief was ready to take some action against Barnabas. She felt she must warn him, but Barnabas would be resting in his coffin in that dark room off the cellar now. And she'd have no opportunity of talking to him until after the performance. That could be too late!

At once she decided on a desperate move. She had a pen and some small sheets of paper in the bag she carried. She'd write a note of warning to the man she loved and deliver it to Hare at the old house. And if Barnabas had told his servant that she knew his secret, it was barely possible that Hare might let her go to him. It was worth a chance.

Instead of going inside and taking the rest she so badly needed when she reached Collinwood, she sat down on one of the garden benches and hastily wrote the warning to Barnabas. In it she explained the chief's reasoning, suggesting that since there was a possibility the chief might send a guard to the theater tonight, it might be better if they didn't plan to meet until the following night after the performance. In the meantime she begged that he'd be careful.

The note written, she carefully folded it and started out for the old house. When she reached it, there wasn't any sign of life. The shutters on the windows were closed and the ancient brick structure seemed deserted. But she knocked loudly on the door until at last she heard footsteps inside. A moment later an angry Hare opened the door a fraction.

She at once held up the note. "For Mr. Collins," she said. "I'm Miss Samson. Please let me to go him."

Hare studied her, and the angry look vanished somewhat from his face. At once she was sure that Barnabas had told him she could be trusted.

She said, "I know. Let me take this to him! It's urgent!"

Hare scowled but he opened the door wide enough for her to enter. She stepped into the shadowed hallway and he slammed the door shut again and bolted it. They were in almost complete darkness now, but she felt sure there was no danger to fear from the faithful Hare.

He clumped down the hall and she followed. When he came to the cellar door he found a candle and holder on a shelf and lit the candle. He held it aloft as he showed her down the worn steps. A moment later they were crossing the musty cellar. At the door of the hidden room she halted.

"I'll go the rest of the way alone," she said. And reached out to take the candle holder.

Hare made a grunting sound and held it away from her.

Her eyebrows raised. She didn't understand the reason for his action. But she opened the door to the room anyway. And then she understood. Barnabas was not resting in darkness. Candles in tall silver candlesticks flickered at both the head and foot of his ornate, oak coffin.

141

Awed by the gloomy room of death she tiptoed in and stood silently by the open coffin. It was the first time she'd ever seen Barnabas in it. He looked very peaceful as if he were merely sleeping. His hands were folded on his breast. All at once she was aware of the clammy chill of the shadowed room.

The flickering candles cast their glow on his calm features. She knew it would be hours before he would awaken, but she wanted him to have the note as soon as he rose from his sleep of the dead. Gently she placed it in one of his hands. The touch of his cold flesh was no different from the coldness she'd noticed before. But with him in the coffin it had a more shocking impact on her.

She felt she could stay there no longer, and she turned and fled from the room, closing the door behind her. Hare was standing outside waiting for her. She gave him a nod of thanks. Then they retraced their steps along the dank, earthern floor of the cellar and up the worn stone steps. In a matter of minutes she was outside in the warm sunshine again and Hare was bolting the door. She was careful to get away from the old house as quickly as she could. She didn't want to take a chance of Chief Haig or any of his men seeing her there.

By the time she returned to Collinwood she only had a half-hour to rest. Next she showered and dressed before going downstairs to dinner. She met Roger and Elizabeth in the hallway and she could see that he was in one of his perturbed moods.

He was telling Elizabeth, "That fellow Haig was back here again today. Another of the graves has been dug up and he's about to make a charge against Barnabas."

Elizabeth was distressed. "Barnabas can't have had anything to do with it."

Roger scowled. "Just the same it took all my persuasion to have him postpone action against our respected cousin for a few days. You must get him to leave."

Then the two noticed Diana and ended the discussion at once. But all through dinner the overheard conversation troubled Diana. It confirmed what she already had known. Chief Haig had decided that Barnabas was to blame for all the unpleasant happenings at Collinwood. She ate silently and paid little attention to the conversation of the others.

The second night's performance was just as well attended as the first had been, but it lacked the excitement and glamor of the previous evening. Diana felt the ballet went just as well. Peter Norrad was as strange as ever backstage, but when he went out to dance he was almost back to his former style.

During the intermission, Alex Carter came to her dressing room. Had she known who it was she wouldn't have opened the door, but once she did, he boldly entered the room in his arrogant way.

She stood by the open door and told him, "I'm in a hurry. I have a change of costume and make-up for the second act."

Alex seemed uneasy. "Why have you been avoiding me lately?" he asked.

"I don't think I have."

"You've been acting differently for the past ten days," he insisted. "I thought we might be good friends at one time. I always preferred you to Mavis."

This annoyed her. "That's easy to say now that Mavis is dead."

Carter's face took on a flush. "You're like the others," he said angrily. "You blame me for what happened to Mavis."

"I think you helped bring it about!"

He stared at her. "And that's why you've been so cold lately."

"I haven't time to argue with you now," she said. "If you don't leave at once I'll complain to the stage manager!"

Alex smiled nastily. "No need of that. I never stay where I'm not welcome." And he went out.

She shut the door after him and became aware that she was trembling. That was the way Carter made her react these days. Anger and frustration had combined to thoroughly upset her. He'd wasted a good deal of the intermission time and she was left with only a few minutes to change.

In her scenes with him in the second act she felt he was dancing very badly. A sloppiness had come into his work and he fairly clumped around the stage when his movements should have been light and graceful. This made it

143

hard for her. But for the most part the ballet went well and once again the audience was generous with its applause.

Mary Wentworth came backstage after the final curtain and invited Diana to drive back to Collinwood with her. Roger had arranged to have Matt Morgan come for her every evening. This surprising generosity on Roger's part was a tribute to their talents. They had won him over to support of their project. Diana gladly agreed to accompany the old woman. She had no plans for meeting Barnabas, and she didn't want to linger at the chapel in view of her experience the previous night.

Not until they were seated in the car together did Mary Wentworth delicately broach the subject of the dancing in the second part of the ballet. "Something was wrong tonight," the director said. "The solo you did was fine. But when you danced with Alex you were off."

"I don't think he's trying," she said. "He's annoyed at the way the critics ignored him."

"He can be difficult," Mary admitted. "I think what happened to Mavis hurt him more than most of us realize."

"In his selfish way he was fond of her," Diana said bitterly. "But he has no character or loyalty. I despise him."

The old woman at her side looked upset. "You mustn't dwell on that or it is bound to show in your work together onstage. I'll speak to him and try and get him to improve."

"You've been very patient with him."

"And for an excellent reason," Mary said. "It was he who suggested we have this summer season here and arranged it. I can't forget that."

"I suppose not," Diana said with a deep sigh.

When they got out of the car at the door of Collinwood she stood for a moment to enjoy the night air. There was a full moon and it flooded the countryside with a silver light that made it almost as bright as daylight.

Staring out at the silver of the ocean, she said, "What a wonderful night."

Mary nodded. "It makes me think of a 'Midsummer Night's Dream.' It was one of my favorite ballets. We had

144

a special lighting plan for it that created exactly this kind of magic glow on stage."

"You translate everything in terms of ballet," Diana charged her with a smile, and they went inside.

She felt on edge and stood by her window staring out at the moon reflected on the ocean. She was concerned about Barnabas and beginning to regret that she'd postponed meeting him. She almost wished she'd taken a chance. But Chief Haig had frightened her with his talk of sending a policeman to the theater to watch her.

She decided to take a shower, hoping it might relax her and make sleep come more quickly. As she left her room to go down the hall to the bathroom, Stefan came down the stairs from the floor above. Seeing her, the young composer hurried down the hall to intercept her.

"I want you to see something," he said. He had an excited air.

She halted and stared at him. "What are you talking about?"

"I've just come from the Captain's Walk up on the roof," he told her. "It's a wonderful spot. Gives you a view of the entire estate. And this is an ideal night with the moon so bright."

"I'm about to go to bed," she said. "I'll see it another time."

"You'll never have the view you will tonight," he argued, taking her lightly by the arm. "It won't take more than a few minutes. Come along."

Rather than seem unfriendly she decided to go with him. She had come to like Stefan, though she still didn't completely understand him. He often had enthusiasms like this and wanted to share them.

He led her up the stairs to the next floor and then they took a steep flight of steps which led up to the rooftop and the Captain's Walk. The circular area had a railing around it and offered a fine panoramic view for miles around.

"You see?" Stefan told her as they stepped out into the open.

She stood with her hands on the railing and gazed raptly at the impressive scene. "I see why you were so excited," she said.

"Nights like this are rare," he said. "Even the village stands out clearly." And it did.

Diana moved around the circle so that she was able to spot the old house, the chapel, and the farmhouse beyond; even the narrow roadways were visible. The night was warm for August in Maine and very still.

Stefan came up beside her. "I see something else I think may interest you."

"Really?" She allowed him to lead her to another part of the railing with a view of the lawns and the cliffs beyond.

"Down there," he said, pointing to the cliff path.

Diana stared at the spot he'd indicated and felt a sudden tension as she saw two figures strolling arm in arm along the path. Even at a distance she was able to recognize Eleanor and Barnabas!

CHAPTER TWELVE

"What do you think of your friend Barnabas now?" Stefan asked her.

She turned to him. "Why should this make me feel any differently about him?" She was straining to be casual, though the sight of Barnabas with the dark-haired girl had given her a start. Now she tried to assure herself that he had sought Eleanor out to explain things to her.

"You are loyal to him," Stefan said. "It seems he doesn't worry much about you."

"Is that why you brought me up here?" she asked bitterly.

"Partly," he said. "And partly because I'd like to have some sort of understanding with you. I've told you I'm in love with you. And I think you might learn to care for me if you'd get over this weird infatuation with Barnabas."

"I don't want to discuss that now," she said, turning her back to him. And gazing down at the cliff path again, she noted that Barnabas and the dark girl had vanished.

Stefan took her by the arm and swung her around facing him. "We could have a wonderful future," he insisted. "My ballet is going to be produced in New York. And you could be the star."

Diana shook her head. "I like you, Stefan. Don't try to force things and cause me to change my mind."

"You're still in love with that madman?" he asked incredulously.

"I don't consider Barnabas mad."

"And you'll not even give me consideration?" he demanded.

"I've told you I'm confused. Let's be content to continue as friends. Don't spoil that," she begged him.

Stefan let her go. "He has you under some kind of spell," he said. "This place has tainted us all with its madness." And with an expression of regret he left her and made his way through the center door and down the steps.

She stood there not wanting to trail him down the steps. It had been a difficult moment. She felt it might be best for a time to avoid the young composer as much as she could. At least until she was able to do something for Barnabas. The growing suspicion that Barnabas was responsible for all the strange happenings at Collinwood had reached a dangerous stage.

With a sigh she turned to stare down at the cliff path again. There was no one in sight now. She assumed Barnabas had found her message when he awakened in his casket. Certainly he had not made an appearance at the chapel. It was likely he'd met Eleanor somewhere else later. And his being with her did not have to mean anything sinister.

It could be his unslaked thirst for blood which had made him turn to the blonde Nora the night before had caused him to seek out Eleanor now. Of course, Stefan knew nothing of the curse under which Barnabas existed. But she shared his secret and understood.

Perhaps the best thing would be to persuade Barnabas to leave at once. It would take time to try and find some specialist willing to attempt to cure him. There must be among the many scientists of the world at least one or two who would be concerned with the plight of the handsome man and try to free him of his two centuries' old torment. And she would stand by him until that happy denouement was achieved.

She might have to leave the ballet without notice, but at least she had remained to see the company through the opening night. If they had to use someone else in the part now it would not be so important. With the rave reviews *Roxanna* had received, it should be easy for Mary Wentworth to secure a name dancer of some sort for the role. She might hurt her reputation and future by leaving, but she could not sacrifice Barnabas for her career. She would do what was best for him.

Reaching this decision gave her a certain peace of mind. She would see Barnabas tomorrow night and tell him all these things. She turned to start down the steps when she thought she saw a shadow move behind the central cone of the tower. She at once stood stark still, staring at the spot where she'd seen the flicker of movement. There was nothing there now. At once she breathed a trifle easier. It had been her imagination. The circular Captain's Walk had been empty when she'd come up with Stefan.

It must still be deserted except for herself, but she was wary now as she started for the door leading to the steep steps. She had reached the door and was about to go down when without a warning sound the terrifying hands seized her and dragged her back.

She cried out in terror and tried to free herself. She hadn't a chance. Her unseen assailant gripped her throat, but she managed another scream before her breath was cut off. At the same time she dug at the hands with her nails and struggled. All at once she was released and hurled towards the railing. Her last conscious thought was that she was surely going toppling over.

She was on the floor of the rooftop tower and an earnest-faced Stefan was kneeling beside her. She raised herself on an elbow. "Someone tried to force me over the railing," she told him in a weak voice.

He frowned. "I was back on the second floor when I heard your screams. By the time I got up here you were slumped on the floor here close to the railing."

"And you didn't meet anyone else?"

"No. No one passed me."

She couldn't accept this. He had to be lying. She began to suspect it was he who had attacked her and when he hadn't successfully propelled her over the railing had assumed the role of the rescuer. It was a far-fetched theory, but at least it offered some explanation. He had left her in a fit of angry jealousy.

"I saw a shadow move," she said. "And when I started for the door, hands seized me."

"I shouldn't have left you up here alone," he said.

She studied him. He seemed sincere enough, and yet she wondered. "They were powerful hands," she said. "I had no chance against them."

"Do you feel well enough to stand?"

"Yes. I'm all right," she said as he assisted her to her feet.

149

He glanced around the circular Captain's Walk. "If anyone was hiding up here they must have kept concealed in the shadows of the stairway until after I left."

"There wouldn't be that much room," she said.

"Room enough if you pressed close to the wall," he told her. "It would seem someone wants to murder you."

"Who?"

He shrugged. "That had better be left to the police."

"They'll only try to blame it on Barnabas, as they do everything else. And you know we saw him far away on the path."

Stefan looked grim. "I'd say he was safe enough this time. We can't blame him for what happened up here."

Diana gave him a knowing look. "It could be one of Collinwood's ghosts. They seem to resent our intrusion."

"I'm almost willing to agree, since I saw no one."

She gave a tiny shiver. "Let's go back down."

He escorted her to her own door. Even then he seemed worried about leaving her. "Better take a look inside before I go," he advised.

"I'll be all right," she promised, but at his insistence she did open the door and check her room. It was just as she'd left it, so she said goodnight to him and went on in.

At once she was presented with another problem. Chief Haig had made it clear he wanted her to immediately advise him if she had any other strange experiences. Surely what had taken place up in the Captain's Walk had been strange enough.

Previously she had held back from keeping the shrewd chief up-to-date on what was going on because she feared he would place the blame for any reported incident on Barnabas. But this time she had Stefan as a witness that Barnabas was a distance away on the estate when she was attacked. It could do the man she loved good if she made an instant report of the bizarre episode.

On the other hand it would bring the police to Collinwood again and Roger Collins would resent that. Caught between her desire to help Barnabas, her fear for her own safety, and the wish to protect the Collins family, she paced up and down for at least ten minutes before she made up her mind to go down to the lower hallway and make the phone call.

150

The old mansion was deathly quiet as she slowly made her way down to the phone. Only a night light dispelled the shadows of the high-ceilinged hall. She stood in the semi-darkness for a long moment, staring up at the fine portrait of Barnabas and wondering where he might be. Then she went to the phone on a small table beneath the stairs and dialed for the operator.

In a low voice she said, "I'd like to speak to the Ellsworth police."

"I'll get you the number," the night operator said.

Diana stood there in the shadows, waiting and growing more nervous every minute. At last, after considerable clicking, the phone rang at the other end, and a male voice answered.

"I'd like to speak to Chief Haig," she said.

"He's gone for the night," the man at the police station said. "Is it urgent?"

"Not that urgent," she said. "Would you please tell him Miss Samson called and ask him to get in touch with me."

"I'll leave a note on his desk for when he arrives in the morning," the man promised.

She thanked him and put the phone down. As she moved out into the main hallway again, she was confronted by a menacing figure blocking her way. Peter Norrad stood there in the shadows, and there was something about him that sent a chill through her.

"I didn't see you at first," she said.

"You were calling the police?" he asked in a dull voice.

"Yes." She tried to hide her nervousness.

"They'll do you no good," Peter said, still between her and the steps.

"I had a message for Chief Haig," she said in a voice betraying a small tremor.

Peter's eyes burned into her. "The police can't help you any more than they could have helped Mavis."

"I don't know what you mean," she faltered.

"What is going on here is beyond human understanding," he said. "Phantoms rule this place. And they'll deal with you as they did with my wife."

She felt it better to agree with him. "It is an eerie old house."

"We understand each other," he said.

151

"I hope so," she told him. Though she only knew that he must be verging on madness or perhaps had been drinking. She heard that he sometimes did drink too much. At any rate, she only wanted to get by him and escape to her room upstairs. She took a tiny step forward.

"Mavis is better dead," Peter said.

"It was a tragedy," she murmured.

"Not really," he insisted. "Many of us would be better dead."

"I have a headache," she apologized. "I must go to my room."

He surprised her by stepping aside to let her pass. She brushed by him with her heart pounding, and not until she was up the first flight of stairs and on her way to her room did she feel safe.

The following morning it was raining again, fog hovered over the ocean. Diana was late going down to breakfast and the only one left at the table was Eleanor. She at once noticed the dark-haired girl was in a somber mood.

Helping herself from the buffet on the sideboard Diana greeted her with, "We finally have a miserable day."

Eleanor looked up from her coffee. "Yes. It is wet."

"And what a surprise after last night," Diana said sitting down across from the other girl. "Such lovely moonlight."

"I didn't pay much attention to it," Eleanor said morosely.

Diana thought she should let her know she'd seen her with Barnabas. She said, "I went up to the Captain's Walk. And I saw you and Barnabas together on the cliff path."

Eleanor showed embarrassment. "Yes. We were together for a while."

Diana searched the girl's neck and despite the poor light in the dining room was sure she saw the usual crimson mark left by Barnabas. Not wanting to stare too obviously, she returned her attention to buttering her toast.

"What did he have to say?" she asked.

Eleanor made a vague gesture. "We talked about a lot of things. I can't really remember all of them. I think he's going away soon."

"Oh?"

The dark girl smiled forlornly. "I received the im-

152

pression that he prefers a bachelor's life." Finishing her coffee, she got up from the table and left the room.

Diana was satisfied. There could be no doubt that Barnabas had spoken plainly to Eleanor. He might not have gone into the details of their romance, but at least he'd clearly discouraged the dark-haired girl from being interested in him.

She was still at the breakfast table when she heard a car drive up in front of Collinwood. A moment or so later the bell rang and Elizabeth answered it. Diana recognized Chief Haig's voice as he asked to speak with her. Then Elizabeth came to the doorway of the dining room.

"You have a visitor," she said, looking somewhat puzzled.

Diana got up hurriedly. "Yes. I phoned the chief last night."

When she went out to the hall, he was standing waiting for her in a dripping plastic raincoat, his battered hat in his hand. His weathered face with the prominent nose wore a grim look.

"You called me?" he said.

"Yes. Something happened I thought you should know."

"I see," he said, and he glanced at Elizabeth, who was still standing there. "Some place Miss Samson and I can chat in private?" he asked.

"The study," she said, and led them down the corridor to it.

The chief stood aside for Diana to enter the paneled room with its book-lined walls. Then he closed the door after them and asked, "Well, what's the latest?"

She quickly told him, ending with, "Once again I didn't see who it was. But I'm sure it wasn't Barnabas Collins."

He smiled wryly. "Don't expect I'd have heard anything about it if you'd thought it was him. He seems to have a way with females."

Diana blushed. "You asked me to inform you if I had any more trouble.

Chief Haig looked resigned. "I guess I'd put somebody trying to murder you under the column of trouble."

"You're ruling out that it could be a ghost," she said.

"Yep," he said. "I'm ruling that out. Those phantom stories have been used to cover up too much here at Collinwood. I'm looking for a flesh and blood killer."

"And you do think Mavis was murdered?"

"I figure she must have been," he said, his shrewd eyes studying her. "And whoever was in the chapel and killed her thinks you saw them. That's why you're on the list."

"But I can't identify them!" she protested.

"They're not certain of that," he said. "Nor are you. One of these days something may turn up and you'll be able to connect it with the murder. The whole thing could click in your mind and you'd know who it was."

"I doubt it," she said.

"I've known it to happen," the chief replied. "The problem is, how am I going to protect you? You're one of those females like you see on television, who are always sticking their necks out for trouble. Either going alone into a haunted house or wandering down some lonely road when they know sure as shootin' there's a murderer loose."

"I'm not quite that bad," she said with a rueful smile.

"Don't pat yourself on the back," he snapped. "There are a lot of women seem to enjoy gettin' into trouble and those television stories don't exaggerate as much as you'd think."

"I've tried to be careful."

"Not that I've noticed," he said. "You shouldn't have stayed up there on that Captain's Walk alone. Not a bit of sense in that!"

"I was sure it was deserted," she faltered.

"In my business we're never sure of anything," Chief Haig said. "And you might be wise to go along with that idea."

"I'm sorry I've been so much trouble."

"Big headache is you never come up with anything for me to work on. I've just about got all this charged up to a crazy Barnabas Collins when you give me a story about being attacked and proof Collins wasn't anywhere near. It's not helpful."

She saw now why he was so upset. His theory about Barnabas had been destroyed. "It's the truth," she pointed out.

"And I'll tell you another truth," the irate chief said.

154

"I'm sorry Collinwood comes under my district!" He left after giving her some strong warnings not to expose herself to any more danger, emphasizing that she shouldn't remain alone anywhere.

It was Saturday night and in spite of the continuing rain there was a good crowd in attendance and the performance went well. Diana had arranged to drive back to the main house with Mary Wentworth, but while she was removing her make-up there was a knock on her door and it was Barnabas.

Her face brightened. "I'm glad you've come!" she greeted him. "I'm so anxious to talk to you."

"I'll wait for you backstage," he promised.

She hurried to finish changing and then let Mary Wentworth know that Barnabas was there waiting for her. After this she joined him in the shadows near the exit.

"It's not raining now," he informed her. "But the fog is heavier."

"Just so long as there isn't a downpour," she said.

They strolled towards Collinwood along the deserted, fog-shrouded lane and he listened with a serious expression as she brought him up-to-date on all that had happened.

"I think we should leave together at once," she suggested. "It doesn't matter whether I stay here now or not."

Barnabas looked unhappy. "We'd be running away from an unsolved murder," he told her. "Leaving too many things unexplained."

"I don't care. I'm only concerned about your safety," she argued.

"Let me worry about that," he said.

"What can we do?" she asked, her tone despairing. "The attempts on my life are coming more often. And Chief Haig still would like to shift all the blame on you!"

As they neared Collinwood he said, "I have come upon some valuable information which I think will be helpful. Now, there is no performance at the chapel tomorrow night since it is Sunday."

"No," she said, wondering what importance this might have.

155

"I want you to meet me at the chapel at dusk," Barnabas told her. "I don't care what the weather is like. Just be sure and be there."

"Why at the chapel?"

He smiled grimly. "I have my reasons. And I want you to drop the word that you're going there to the others at Collinwood. Be sure everyone knows you're meeting me there at dusk."

She frowned. "Couldn't that be dangerous?"

"Not tomorrow night," he told her as they came to a halt before the entrance to the mansion. "And who knows? Perhaps the mysterious ghost will favor us with another visit?"

She decided not to question him about it any further. She was sure he was much wiser in these things than she would ever be. It troubled her that he refused to discuss any plans for their future, but she forgot some of her worries in the tenderness of his embrace as he kissed her goodnight.

Sunday was another rainy day, but the downpour had tapered off to a series of sudden, heavy showers. Still, it was a drab day, during which the various people in the big house became restless. As the afternoon waned Diana was careful to follow out the instructions Barnabas had given her. She let it be known that she was meeting Barnabas even if the bad weather continued.

By the time dinner was over she felt everyone at Collinwood had heard of her intentions. Mary Wentworth had even asked her to go into the box office when she was there and bring back a bundle of mail that had been left there on Saturday.

Stefan intercepted her in the front hall as she was leaving in rain hood and coat. The young composer said, "Aren't you being a little too daring going to the chapel alone on a night like this?"

"I'll be all right," she promised.

"I wonder," he said. "I suppose if you're determined to do something foolish you'll do something foolish."

She gave him a faint smile in return and went on out. It was raining just a little and was certainly a dreadful evening. The fog had settled in thickly once more and the lane was filled with puddles. She tried to pick her way so she wouldn't get her feet soaking wet.

Only her confidence in Barnabas had given her the courage to make this trip to the chapel. It would be deserted and there wouldn't even be many of the boys and girls of the company at the nearby farmhouse. They all tried to drive off somewhere on their free days.

Darkness was at hand as she reached the chapel. She stood there hesitantly, hoping that Barnabas would put in an appearance. She'd thought he might be there waiting for her but he wasn't. As she remained there in the forbidding dark of the wet night she began to experience a growing uneasiness—an uneasiness that bordered on terror.

She decided to use the keys Mary had given her and go inside and get the letters from the box office. Her nerves barely under control, she fumbled with the key in the lock and took much too long to get the door open. The blackness inside increased her fear as she groped towards the small cubicle built as a ticket office. She was about to turn on the light in there when the bell in the chapel tower above began to toll.

The shock of it froze her where she stood. Visions of the ghost of Mario, the mysterious ghost, raced across her mind. Knowing that the bell tolling signaled a death, and remembering that she was marked to die, she realized with horror she had walked into a trap. Where was Barnabas? What could have delayed him?

The tolling of the bell ended but its doleful echo lingered in her mind. Then new terror came to her when she heard shuffling footsteps coming towards her as she stood halfway in the entrance to the ticket office. With a cry of fear she ran across the chapel to the narrow, winding stairs leading to the tower. All she could think of was escaping from the unknown horror stalking her.

As she raced up the worn stone steps she sobbed and gasped out her terror. And she was vaguely conscious of being followed. Reaching the tower she stumbled and fell on the rough floor boards. Before she could lift herself up the thing was upon her. The merciless grip of those hands she had become so familiar with but had never seen closed on her throat. She knew there was no way of escape. This was to be the moment of her death!

As consciousness slipped away from her she became
157

aware of another presence in the small tower room, and the pressure eased on her throat as a struggle went on above her. There was the blinding gleam of a heavy flashlight and the sound of male voices.

Chief Haig's familiar voice came clearly over the others. "All right! We've got him!"

Then the strong light was flashed in her face and she saw the anxious features of Barnabas as he gazed down at her. "Sorry it took so much time," he said. And with irony in his voice, he added, "We've got our mysterious ghost and he turns out not to be invisible."

The plain face of Chief Haig came into the picture. "He's right," the chief said. "We've got our killer. Your dancing partner, Alex Carter."

After that they took her back to Collinwood, and when she was comfortably in bed Barnabas came up to fill her in on all that she had missed. In the melee she hadn't even seen Carter. They'd carted him off to a waiting car while she'd been coming around.

Barnabas sat at her bedside, and with a relieved expression on his handsome face, said, "It was when I visited the Blue Whale one night that I learned Hank had been in there. And one of the regulars had recognized him as an ex-convict who'd served time in the state prison. They also mentioned seeing him with one of the members of your ballet company."

"Alex Carter."

"Yes. The description fitted him," Barnabas said. "I passed the information on to Chief Haig. And he soon rounded this Hank fellow up. He'd been hiding in one of the Collinwood barns. Hank talked and admitted that he and Carter were working together."

"Doing what?"

"Some years ago," Barnabas explained, "a couple of bank robbers hid the sizable proceeds of a hold-up at Collinwood. They buried the money in a metal box in a grave in the old cemetery. Hank heard about it in prison and when he came out contacted Carter, a crony from carnival days, and suggested they try and locate the money."

Diana nodded. "And that is why Carter encouraged Mary Wentworth to bring the ballet troupe here. So he and Hank could carry on the search."

"Exactly," Barnabas said. "Hank was to get a handyman job here. But he got drunk and spoiled that. So he had to work undercover from then on. He had no idea which grave the money was in, so he began to dig up them all. In the meantime Mavis found out what Carter and the ex-convict were up to and threatened to tell Elizabeth unless they cut her in on the money."

"And Carter killed her to silence her?"

"Yes. And thought you might have seen him as he escaped, so he felt he had to kill you. The ironical thing about it all is the money hasn't been found and I doubt that it ever will be." Barnabas smiled grimly. "It has turned out to be as elusive as the ghost of Mario."

She sighed. "That's over with. What about you? Now we must decide to leave. While Chief Haig is in good humor and has forgotten all the other incidents of the girls with the crimson mark on their throats."

Barnabas smiled at her sadly. "I'm not forgetting about that," he promised her. "First I want you to get a good night's rest. We'll meet after the performance tomorrow night and discuss the future." And he leaned over to gently touch his lips to hers.

Monday was a day of problems. Tom, the young man with the curly hair, had been understudying Alex Carter and now had to move into his part. This meant a long day of rehearsals by a company tense from the revelations of Sunday night.

But the ballet went on before the usual packed house on Monday. And Diana felt the new young man did very well. She was eagerly waiting the final curtain so she could join Barnabas. His vagueness about himself the previous night had left her uneasy.

Stefan was already at the piano playing the overture for the second part of the ballet when she took her place in the wings for her entrance. The young composer had begun the lovely waltz tune that was to make him famous, when the stage manager came up to her and touched her arm.

"You've got a few minutes, so I thought I might as well give this to you now," he whispered. "Delivered by messenger just now."

She thanked him and took it, staring at her name written in a graceful hand in black ink on the parchment envelope.

Then she tore the envelope open and drew out the single sheet inside. Written there in the same neat hand was the message: "Goodbye. Barnabas." And that was all!

Tears brimmed in her lovely eyes and she crinkled the sheet up and let it fall. Stefan continued to play the haunting waltz as a prelude to the rising of the curtain. She prepared for her entrance, knowing she would never see Barnabas again and that it never could have been any other way. Yet, whenever she heard this waltz she would remember and for a brief moment he would fill her heart.